TIME HUNTER

THE WINNING SIDE
by LANCE PARKIN

TIME HUNTER

THE WINNING SIDE
by LANCE PARKIN

First published in England in 2003 by Telos Publishing Ltd
61 Elgar Avenue, Tolworth, Surrey, KT5 9JP, England • www.telos.co.uk

Telos Publishing Ltd values feedback. Please e-mail us with any comments you
may have about this book to: feedback@telos.co.uk

ISBN: 1-903889-35-9 (paperback)
The Winning Side © 2003 Lance Parkin.
ISBN: 1-903889-36-7 (deluxe hardback)
The Winning Side © 2003 Lance Parkin.
Time Hunter format © 2003 Telos Publishing Ltd. Honoré Lechasseur and
Emily Blandish created by Daniel O'Mahony.

The moral rights of the author have been asserted.

Typeset and Printed in England by TTA Press
5 Martins Lane, Witcham, Ely, Cambs, CB6 2LB, England • www.ttapress.com

2 3 4 5 6 7 8 9 10 11 12 13 14 15

British Library Cataloguing in Publication Data.
A catalogue record for this book is available from the British Library

TIME HUNTER

THE WINNING SIDE
by LANCE PARKIN

PROLOGUE

One in the morning under Hammersmith Bridge has always looked the same and will always look the same.

Always black silt, always the slow, grey Thames. The warehouses on the opposite bank could have been built derelict, their windows glazed and smashed the same day by the same men, as bricklayers set fires against the walls before their cement was dry. Before the bridge, before man, megalosaurs must have come down to the mud banks to drink, their calls like the foghorns here tonight. Their bones lie under the mud, below the shards of flint, below the discarded Roman coins and the pieces of Tudor pottery.

And then, on a cool, crisp, December night – for the merest moment – something happened that had never been seen before.

The woman and the man were suddenly there, with just the faintest crackle of blue light.

After that, there was nothing unusual to see. She was dressed in thin, drab overalls that were too large, and overwhelmed her slight figure. She had long, chestnut hair. Her name was Emily Blandish. He was broad, shaven-headed; his suit had been made for him, and it just about looked like it. This was Radford.

There was a moment or two between their arrival and the murder. Radford looked around, sniffed the air. If he noticed that Emily Blandish was shivering, he gave no sign of it.

'We're here?' he asked. 'We could be anywhere. You're sure we're here?'

'We're here,' she told him.

'How can you tell?'

'I don't know. But I can. It feels right.'

Radford shifted, leaving a fresh footprint. It hadn't occurred to him until that moment that there would be a set of tracks leading back to the shore, but no tracks down here. If anyone noticed that, they'd assume they'd arrived by boat. But that would have left impressions in the mud, too. Would that pique someone's curiosity? Lead them to ask questions?

The mud was already sucking itself flat where his first footprints had been, the evidence erasing itself.

And so he broke the woman's neck, watched her drop into the mud, and left her alone under Hammersmith Bridge.

CHAPTER 1

Honoré Lechasseur wasn't the ideal man for this job.

A suspicious wife wanted to find out why her husband was a couple of hours late coming home on Tuesdays, and sometimes Thursdays. The husband was a man of routine, but recently that routine had changed. He was a civil servant, and the wife had rung his office one evening when he was running late, only to be told he'd left on time. When he'd returned, he'd lied, said he'd been held up at the office. He was already secretive about his work, as civil servants are wont to be, even to their wives. Rather than just ask him, the wife had let this carry on for a month, then another month. She suspected him, of course, but found it easier to hire a detective to follow him than simply talk to him.

She was a customer of Mr Syme, a bookseller on Charing Cross Road. She knew, vaguely, that Syme had 'contacts'. Perhaps the two of them had been discussing detective fiction, and he had let slip that he knew a detective or two.

Lechasseur wasn't a detective. There wasn't really a word to describe what he did. 'Spiv' came closest, but he wasn't that. He preferred 'fixer'. Four years after the war had ended, the skyline was full of cranes as the bombsites became buildings again, but London still hadn't been put back the way it had been. People had moved out and not returned, rationing was still in place, priorities had changed, some of the old trading routes no longer existed. There was a new society being formed, right here at the heart of Empire. With rationing, everyone ate the same.

In military service, the social classes met, even if they never quite mixed. The government were building a new state, 'the welfare state', where everyone went to the same hospitals, travelled in the same railway carriages, went to the same schools. Lechasseur had seen a gap in the market, seen a niche for himself. For a price, he could find the little luxuries that the shops were always running out of. He had contacts. The natives couldn't see past the new buildings, the new spirit. It took an outsider, like Lechasseur, a black man who qualified as an outsider even in his native Louisiana, to see that London was still London, that not everything had changed. What he hadn't predicted, but was obvious in retrospect, was that his knowledge would quickly prove to be his most valuable commodity. Plenty of people knew how things were meant to work, like the Underground train system, or the drains, or the police, or the insurance companies. Lechasseur was one of the few people who knew what really made the heart of the city beat.

Until recently, that had been enough. He wasn't a rich man, but he was making a living. What he did wasn't run-of-the-mill, but it wasn't illegal. He liked London, maybe because it was big and dirty and complicated enough that you could make it your own, whoever you were. It was a big pond; there was room for plenty of small fish.

Then he'd met Emily Blandish.

People who knew what they were talking about had called him a 'time sensitive'. He'd had an accident that had damaged his mind. Or perhaps it had fixed it. Now he saw things in a different way. As yet, he wasn't sure what else it meant.

Except his eyes had been opened, his horizons had been broadened, and he knew he shouldn't just be here, playing detective for some friend of a bookseller.

Lechasseur was in a side road in sight of the British Museum. He'd followed Brown, the errant husband, a few stops down the Northern Line from his office. Like the fool he was, Lechasseur had brought his bicycle with him. Being a black man tall enough that his head poked through the jostle of commuters with a long leather coat – the only one like it on this side of the Atlantic – and a distinctive fedora, just wasn't enough. He had to bring a bicycle with him, struggle down and up the crowded wooden escalators with it. That way, Lechasseur was truly unique, almost impossible to miss or forget seeing. Brown was on foot, so Lechasseur was only pushing the thing around anyway; he wasn't riding it.

But incredibly, Brown hadn't seen him. Lechasseur guessed it didn't even occur to most people that they could be being followed. He wasn't sure what Brown did in the civil service – even Mrs Brown was unclear on that point – but Lechasseur hoped it wasn't something that depended on intuition or observation, or it would be a while longer before the country got back on its feet.

An hour ago, Brown had stopped abruptly at one of the doors facing onto the street, just to the side of an antiques shop, and pressed the second – third? – doorbell. Then the door had opened, and he'd gone in, and presumably upstairs. Lechasseur was left outside. The evening was dark, but only the first floor curtains were closed. The lights were on behind them. So, don't assume anything, but assume Brown's gone up into the first floor flat above – directly above? – the shop.

This was Bloomsbury, a part of London that Lechasseur knew little about. He'd never even been to the Museum. He had vague associations – writers lived here. The flat didn't look like much from the street, but some of these terraces were deceptively large. This was an expensive place to live.

Lechasseur had propped his bicycle against the shop front and gone into the shop. Whatever Brown was doing, he was doing it about ten feet above Lechasseur's head. Don't assume anything, but assume he's at least half-naked by now.

The plan was to feign interest in antiques, and hope the shop was open for a while longer this evening, then make a note of when Brown left. In practice, Lechasseur had one eye making sure no-one was trying to steal his bicycle.

'Sir?' the shopkeeper asked.

A small, youngish man.

Objects, all objects, had height and depth and breadth and . . . anotherth. It was only Lechasseur who could see that fourth direction, but he couldn't always see it, he couldn't control what he saw.

Here, surrounded by antiques, he felt a little dizzy, almost like he was drunk. Each pot, each statue, each coin spiralled back through time. So much history in the room, and he could see it all.

'Sir?' the shopkeeper – too young to serve in the War, was at

Cambridge, a minor public school before that, the third son of a . . . – said, and Lechasseur snapped out of his reverie.

Lechasseur smiled what was meant to be a disarming smile, but he knew it probably just added to the impression that he was drunk.

'Does that interest you, sir?' the shopkeeper said, but what he meant was *are you in here just to shelter from the cold?*

'That's Roman,' Lechasseur told him, pointing at a brooch. 'Made in Britain, I mean, but during the Roman occupation.'

'It was made in France, sir. Gaul. Imported here.'

'England,' Lechasseur assured him. 'Bath. 318 AD. From Cornish gold.'

The shopkeeper smiled indulgently. 'It's fourth century, sir, yes.'

A door closed outside, and Lechasseur spun round.

Brown walked straight past the shop window, head down. Ten minutes – Lechasseur confirmed that with a quick glance at his watch. He'd been expecting Brown to stay up there longer than that. He felt almost embarrassed for him.

'Going?' the shopkeeper was asking, a little redundantly, given that Lechasseur was already outside and had one hand on his bike. Brown was turning the corner. Lechasseur hesitated – rather than follow him, no doubt back to the Underground, and then off home, there was another choice: he could ring the doorbell. Brown had left alone, so the woman – Lechasseur presumed it was a woman – would be in.

He looked back inside the antiques shop. It was almost freezing outside, but back in there it was warm, inviting. British shops were often like that – the proprietor appearing more keen to talk to his customers than do anything so vulgar as sell things to them. Syme's bookshop was the same – Lechasseur had spent hours in there, just talking. Then he'd leave, and having bought three books, two of which he'd never have dreamt of buying if left to his own devices. He realised that the shopkeeper hadn't been trying to get him out of his shop just now; he'd simply been trying to start a conversation.

He'd better follow Brown, before he found himself spending ten pounds on a Roman oil lamp.

Brown had, as Lechasseur predicted, headed straight home. Once he was sure of that, Lechasseur had returned to his own place. He had the address of the flat in Bloomsbury that Brown was frequenting, and tomorrow he'd follow that lead. He'd done enough for one day.

There were a couple of uniformed policemen waiting for him.

Lechasseur realised that his lips were dry, and tried to suppress any reaction, knowing they'd be looking for any sign of panic. If they'd searched his place, they would have found the last box of smuggled cigars, nothing more. There were, of course, any number of past misdemeanours that might have come to their attention.

Then he saw that they were the ones hiding something. Their grave expressions. One of them removed his helmet.

'Honoré Lechasseur?'

If they had a description of him, any description at all, they must have known who he was. This was no time for a cocky 'Who wants to know?'

'Yes, that's right.'

The policeman nodded. 'You're a friend of Miss Emily Blandish?'

'I suppose I am.' He hadn't known her very long, but they were friends.

'What's the nature of your relationship?'

'We're friends, like you said.'

Neither of those observations was a question, but Lechasseur found himself shaking his head anyway.

'Her landlady said you were the nearest thing she had.' The policeman was trying to be discreet.

'We've been through a lot together.'

'Care to explain?'

'I helped her out.'

They wanted more.

'She was found on a bombsite,' Lechasseur explained. 'She'd lost her memory. She was wearing pyjamas, she didn't have anything that could identify her, none of the locals recognised her. But she spoke English, she knew her name. Once the doctors had finished with her, she was discharged and . . . well . . . she had nowhere to go. I tried to find out more about her.'

Failed, too, Lechasseur didn't add. And he'd pleased himself with how straightforward he'd made it all sound – amazing how missing a few little details out made Emily's life story sound almost normal.

'She has no relatives,' the other policeman said. 'No family.'

'That's my understanding,' Lechasseur confirmed.

The policeman looked at him with such pity that Lechasseur was suddenly terrified.

'She was discovered this morning, sir. Please could you come with us. We need someone to identify the body, and it looks like you're our best candidate.'

He knew it really was Emily before they pulled back the sheet.

Don't worry about how she died, yet, he told himself. Let's see the evidence, let's poke a finger into the wounds.

'Ready?' the pathologist asked, not waiting for Lechasseur to nod.

She was naked. He hadn't expected that, and found himself staring at her. She was older than you'd think from looking at her. She was in her mid-twenties, but looked almost adolescent. She was even more slight without her clothes. He'd seen corpses before, in Normandy. They hadn't been as intact or scrubbed clean as this, but he recognised the colour, or rather the lack of it in the lips, the skin, the nipples. Her brown hair was just as vivid, though. It was meant to keep growing after death – a myth, he'd read somewhere; something to do with the skin contracting as it stiffened.

They'd closed her eyes, laid her out, arms at her side.

He tried looking at the body another way, the way only he could. He'd see her history, he'd see who had done this to her, and then he'd find him and kill him.

Lechasseur brushed his hand against Emily's stomach. It was cold, stiff, like a side of meat, not a person. Could you get used to seeing human beings like this? It wasn't normal. Even the War, and all those millions of dead bodies, hadn't changed that, thank God. But a young girl like this . . . someone who could reasonably have expected to live to see the twenty-first century. How could that be anything but a crime against history?

The pathologist was looking at him sternly.

Lechasseur guessed it wasn't the done thing to touch her. But if he wanted to *see* it, then it often helped to touch.

Not this time. Damn this – he could tell the life story of a Roman brooch, but not her, not when it mattered.

'Is it Miss Blandish?' he was asked, in what passed for a gentle tone.

'Yes,' Lechasseur said. He hesitated for a moment.

'No,' a familiar voice chipped in.

Emily Blandish was standing in the doorway.

'I was running that errand for you all afternoon. I got home and everyone looked like they'd seen a – '

She'd seen the body, and couldn't finish the sentence.

The pathologist was puzzled. 'You have a twin?' he asked.

'No . . .'

'You don't sound sure.'

'Miss Blandish doesn't know much about her past,' Lechasseur told him. 'It's a long story.'

The pathologist held up his hand. 'Of course. I remember the papers – knew I recognised the body from somewhere.'

Emily was oblivious to everything but the corpse.

'It isn't me.'

'Of course not, my dear. A terrible way to discover you had a sister, but – '

'Where was she found?'

'Under Hammersmith Bridge. Early this morning.'

'You cleaned her up, then?' said Lechasseur. He should have noticed the smell of soap before.

'She was covered in mud.'

'And naked?' Emily asked.

'She was wearing overalls. They're in the other room.'

'Just overalls?' Lechasseur asked.

'What do you mean?'

'No jewellery?' Lechasseur elaborated.

'I don't own any jewellery.'

'No jewellery. No personal effects. Not even underwear.'

Emily was blushing.

'This isn't you,' Lechasseur reminded her.

'How could it be?' the pathologist agreed. 'Oh wait . . . there was a watch. A wristwatch.'

Lechasseur asked if they could see it and the pathologist left the room. They were bent over the body before the door was closed behind him.

'She's my twin,' Emily told him. She seemed remarkably unaffected by seeing, to all intents and purposes, her own body. If she was uncomfortable at Lechasseur seeing her . . . it . . . naked, she didn't register that, either.

'She has the same length hair.' Lechasseur observed. Emily's hair was slightly longer than the fashion this year.

'We need something more than that. Look here. The same mole.' A tiny mole on both their necks. 'Do twins have exactly the same moles?'

'I don't know,' Lechasseur admitted. He was getting a little uncomfortable.

'I don't have those bruises on my neck and shoulder.'

'Your neck hasn't been broken. That was how she died. That's why it's bruised.'

'You can tell that by looking at her?'

'I can.'

'The bruise on the shoulder.'

'Looks nasty, and older than the ones on the neck. Have you got a bruised shoulder?'

Emily shook her head. 'But I don't think twins have the same moles. Are there any other differences? Her nails are shorter. Oh . . . '

'What?'

She held up the body's hand. A half-inch cut on the tip of the ring finger.

She held up her own hand. A half-inch cut on the tip of the ring finger.

'We both cut ourselves slicing bread. Same finger.'

The twin's wound was slightly more ragged, slightly more puckered. Just like Emily's would have been, if it had got wet.

Lechasseur shook his head. 'It's a trick.'

'A trick?'

'Someone's trying to scare you.'

'He's starting to succeed. And he's gone to a lot of trouble. This isn't someone who looks a bit like me – if I had a twin, this body would look more like me than she did. Do you know how they did that?'

Lechasseur had to concede that he didn't. He'd heard about criminals substituting one body for another, but it was a crude trick. You got a body the same sort of height and age and colouring. Then you set fire to it, or mutilated it, because it didn't matter how similar the body looked, it wouldn't fool even an acquaintance in the cold light of day. The whole idea was that everyone thought it was an accident and stopped asking questions.

'Can't you *see* anything?' Emily asked.

'No. I could see the pathologist. I can see you. I can see you cutting yourself. It wasn't bread, it was bacon.'

'Hey . . . yes, you're right. But you get nothing from this . . . thing? From her?'

Lechasseur shook his head.

'If they hadn't scrubbed the body, then we might have found something.'

Lechasseur was examining the notes. 'Hammersmith Bridge. Time of death last night, around midnight. No sign of a struggle.'

'I should make sure I stay away from Hammersmith Bridge last night, and that I don't wear overalls.'

'You don't own any –' She gave him a pointed look. 'Women do. They used to in the munitions factories. I bet they still do if they work in the docks, or . . .'

'She wasn't wearing underwear,' she reminded him. 'I . . . well, I wouldn't. I just wouldn't go out.'

She looked down at the small, naked body, and for the first time she looked upset.

'This isn't you,' he assured her.

'It is, Honoré. Look at it. Somehow, it is.'

It was. And Honoré Lechasseur had to admit it was a much more interesting mystery than what a civil servant was doing that took him away from his wife and to Bloomsbury.

As far as the police were concerned, there wasn't anything to investigate. This was nothing but a coincidence, they said. Lechasseur and Emily made their way back to his flat. They'd even let them keep the dead girl's watch – or, more precisely, they hadn't noticed when Lechasseur slipped it into his pocket. It was, predictably enough, the exact make that Emily wore, a cheap watch she'd bought in the East End. The dead girl's had stopped at one – presumably damaged as its owner had been swallowed by the mud and water.

'A man with two watches never knows the correct time,' Emily said.

'What?'

'Something I read,' she said. 'I can't remember who said it.'

'I suppose I should be grateful they didn't think I was a suspect,' Lechasseur noted.

Emily had been nervous all the way home. She had one hand pulled up at the collar of her coat. They'd quickly run through the likely explanations, principally because there weren't that many likely explanations. The best they'd come up with was what the police said: it was all a coincidence.

'If there weren't coincidences, there wouldn't be a word for it,' Lechasseur had said. Hardly profound, and he could tell Emily wasn't buying.

So, exhausting the rational explanations, they'd tried some of the irrational ones. A few weeks after Emily had been found wandering on that bombsite, Emily told Lechasseur, a man had come to her flat to talk about putting her in a book about the unusual. Boys raised by wolves, incredible feats of luck (both good and bad), twins brought up in different parts of the world who meet up and discover they've led parallel lives. The writer had hoped that Emily's story would be a good example, one his publishers liked because it was topical.

'He believed in ghosts and spirits,' she told Lechasseur. 'And he mentioned the idea of a doppelgänger.'

Lechasseur shrugged.

'A double,' she explained. 'A supernatural, exact double. And if you see it, it means you're going to die.'

She was so matter-of-fact about it. This evening had disconcerted her – hell, why wouldn't it have done? But she was trying to think about it, to come up with a solution.

'Whoever that body was, it wasn't supernatural.'

They'd reached his flat, and Lechasseur hesitated, feeling slightly awkward as usual. Emily smiled at him gently. 'It's okay, Honoré, I know this is your space, and I'm grateful – '

At that moment, car doors slammed closed across the road, and two men started coming purposefully towards them. Plain clothes police. If they'd been uniformed, it would hardly have been more obvious.

'Honoré Lechasseur?'

'Yeah, Hi, I was just with you. It was all a mistake – this is Miss Blandish, and as you can see, she's – '

The nearest grabbed him, the other hit him in the stomach.

Lechasseur tried struggling, but the guy holding him was too strong. Another punch.

'Stop that!' Emily cried, trying to prise the guy's arms from around her friend.

The guy let go of Lechasseur and rounded on her. Emily held up her hands, tried to protect herself, but he just brought a heavy blow down on her shoulder, knocked her over.

Lechasseur turned, and would have got a good swing on the guy, if it wasn't for his associate. The other man punched Lechasseur in the back, right in the kidneys. Lechasseur tried to stay upright, but ended up on his knees, not conscious of anything but the pain. He ought to be used to pain by now, but . . .

'Stay away from Simon Brown,' the man who'd hit Emily said.

Then the two of them went back to their car, got in and drove off.

Lechasseur found Emily was offering a hand to him, trying to help him up.

'Do you know – ' she began.

'Never seen them before.'

Had they been following him this afternoon, when he'd been following Brown? Lechasseur knew Brown hadn't seen him. But had someone else? Could those two men have been right behind him on the Tube, at the antiques shop?

Emily winced.

'You okay?' Lechasseur asked.

'Well,' Emily replied quietly, 'at least we know how the body in the morgue got the bruise on her shoulder.'

CHAPTER 2

Emily cooked herself breakfast, using the last of the eggs, which annoyed Lechasseur more than he knew it should have done.

It was good to see her alive. But across London she was lying on a slab. What would they do with the body? A full post mortem, a brief time for some relative to come forward, then a burial, he assumed. Should Lechasseur go? Would they even be informed when it was taking place?

The bruise on Emily's shoulder had developed during the night, and was the same shape as the one on the corpse, she had told him.

He couldn't help but think that the body was Emily. Somehow she had both died and not died. Impossible, of course, but so much of Lechasseur's life in the last few weeks had been impossible. Was there some way in which events could branch off in two directions? Life was a series of choices, some conscious decisions, some accidents. Everyone understood that, at some level. If you flipped a coin, it could come up heads or tails. He knew so little about Emily, but what he knew was that time flowed differently around her. He couldn't explain it any better than that.

She'd just appeared one day on a bombsite. Heads. But had she appeared somewhere else, too? Tails. It would explain the identical bodies. Perhaps there was some explanation for the bruises – some arcane link between the two bodies. Prick one, does the other not bleed? Except that the other Emily had been murdered – if you hit her, and 'his' Emily got the bruise, then why wouldn't her neck break when her twin's did? The prospect that there was some sort of time delay, that Emily's neck would just snap in a day or two worried him . . . but as Emily herself had said, if that was the case, they couldn't do anything.

Lechasseur couldn't help thinking about Scrooge and the Ghost of Christmas Future. Finding the body was a sign, a warning. They were meant to do something differently, or Emily would die. He'd tried explaining this to Emily, who had never read the story or even heard of Charles Dickens. When Lechasseur admitted that he had no idea how Emily was meant to mend her ways to prevent her fate, it joined the pile of useless theories they'd amassed.

Was there a connection between Emily's 'death' and the business with Brown? There was no logical reason to link the two, but Lechasseur couldn't help but try to join the dots. The men who'd given Emily the bruise knew about Simon Brown. Tenuous, but a link.

Lechasseur's first choice of the day was whether or not to carry on following Brown around. The case had always been of minimal interest to him, he didn't fancy the idea of being beaten up again. He was seriously considering just letting it drop.

It was Emily who came up with a solution – the men had warned him to stay away from Simon Brown. He could pursue the case without pursuing the man. Around ten o'clock, he headed back to Bloomsbury, and the flat above the antiques shop.

Four doorbells, one for each of the flats. Not all of them had names next to them. Lechasseur made a guess which was the one for the first floor. Brown had pressed either the second or third. Lechasseur decided on the second.

The latch clicked. There was no way anyone could have made it downstairs in that time – and he'd have heard them, he was sure – so the door had been opened for him. Very trusting.

Lechasseur stepped into a hallway that managed to exude class and a degree of wealth while also being almost bare. The carpet was thick, and Lechasseur found himself wiping his feet automatically oì,the tough doormat before he stepped all the way inside. He made his way up a flight of stairs, his footsteps muffled by the carpet. The door on the first floor was already an inch open. He entered a room full of dark furniture, lined with bookcases.

They were history books, mainly. There were Russian history books (including books with authors with names like Zamiatin), books about trade unions, as well as poetry. There was a small pile of faded newspapers on a side table.

The woman registered no surprise to see him. Lechasseur doubted she would say the same about himself. She was standing in the middle of the room. She was tall, thin, wearing a silk dressing gown that was purple, but had probably faded from a vivid red. She had brown waist-length hair, heavily streaked with grey, but, looking at her, she probably wasn't forty yet. She had a glass of whisky in her hand.

'And you are?' she asked, with one of those impossibly English accents.

Her fingernails were covered in a thick, impeccable varnish that matched the colour of her gown. Lechasseur couldn't be certain, but suspected that the gown and the nail varnish was all she was wearing.

'Honoré Lechasseur.'

'An American.' It couldn't possibly qualify as a question.

'And your name, ma'am?'

She smiled. 'Amanda. And you're too late; he's already come and gone.' She looked at him as she poured a generous measure into one of the three glasses that were out. 'Drink?'

It was ten in the morning, Lechasseur reminded himself. He wondered if 'Amanda' knew what time it was.

'A little early?' she asked, taking a seat. As she sat, the gown parted, revealing a long, very white, leg. She covered it over almost immediately.

Lechasseur hesitated.

'Do I need to remind you that it's you calling on me?' she asked. She didn't seem worried. Was there someone else here, ready for trouble? Lechasseur didn't think so. Amanda must be lucky enough to live safe from the threat of violence. This was, of course, how most people lived. Lechasseur could just remember what that had been like.

'No, ma'am.'

'I can see you're not a stupid man, Mr Lechasseur.'

'You can?'

'The first thing you did was look at the titles of the books,' she told him. 'You've read this?' She passed him a book as she tidied an envelope away into a drawer.

Homage to Catalonia.

'No. I served in the War. I don't like reading about them.'

'You fought in Spain? Is it rude to ask for whom?'

'Ma'am, I meant the last War. I was a GI. I fought in France.'

'You've killed people?'

She didn't seem too interested in the answer, so Lechasseur shrugged.

'Simon Brown,' he said, instead of answering her question.

Amanda cocked her head to one side. 'What about him?'

'You know him?'

'Presumably you know I do; that wasn't just a lucky guess.'

'His wife wonders where he's been spending his evenings.'

'Does she? Why haven't you told her that he spends them here?' She sipped at her whisky. 'I'm surprised they sent an American. I suppose I shouldn't be.'

'They?'

'The government, Mr Lechasseur. The state.'

'I don't work for the government.'

She looked over at him.

'I don't,' he insisted.

'I have no doubt you're not on the payroll. But however you define it – '

Lechasseur cut her off. 'I don't work for the government.'

'You're going to tell me you don't even follow affairs of state.'

If he felt like having the conversation, that's exactly what he'd tell her. He'd lived in London only a few years, he'd not voted in a General Election. He wasn't sure he was entitled to.

'We are living at a crucial time,' she continued.

'Doesn't everyone?' Lechasseur countered.

'Ah – a philosopher.'

'Hardly.'

'But you're wrong. The dust is still settling from the War. Everything was thrown up into the air, we can't yet be certain where it has landed.'

Lechasseur glanced over at her. She was fitting a cigarette at the end of an ivory cigarette holder. As she leant over, Lechasseur got confirmation that she was wearing nothing underneath her robe. She retrieved a ha'penny box of safety matches and struck one against the side. It took a moment to get the cigarette lit. A recent habit, then – or at least the holder was a recent affectation. If it had seen much use, it wouldn't have stayed so white, he reasoned.

Amanda was facing him again, drawing some smoke in.

'The people you work for – please, don't give me that look again – they know this. They think that they've got the power, but it's the power that has them. It works to a new and terrible logic, one they don't understand.'

'Well I sure as hell don't understand,' Lechasseur confessed, a little more candidly than he ought to, were he keeping his cards close to his chest.

'The atom bomb,' Amanda said, as though she'd explained everything in three words. 'You have heard of the atom bomb?'

He looked at her. 'You said yourself I'm not a stupid man.'

She smiled. 'There's a new logic there. A whole new way of fighting a war. Or of not fighting one.'

'It's just a big bomb, ma'am.'

'One atom bomb can destroy a city. And with that power – '

'Ask the people of Coventry or Dresden, and they'll remind you we didn't need atom bombs to do that.' Lechasseur held up his hand. 'Look, lady, I work for Simon Brown's wife. She wants to know if he's got another woman.'

She frowned, clearly not believing his story. 'You're a . . . what do you call them? A private eye?'

'No . . . Well, that is what I'm doing here. But this is a favour for a friend.'

'You're a friend of Simon's wife?'

'Er . . . no. Look . . . I . . . are you . . . ?'

'Of course we are, Mr Lechasseur. I commend you on your resourcefulness. I was led to understand that most detectives snuck around and examined dustbins for discarded receipts and correspondence. You just knocked on my door and asked me. How shall we continue? We've been having an affair for two months. He took me to Brighton once, heaven knows why – I think he thought it was the form. I've had lovers with more flair, but he makes up for that with – '

Lechasseur grimaced, his discomfort making Amanda grin.

'Simon's wife knows already,' the woman continued. 'Of course she does – she may not admit it, but where does she think he is in the evenings, for heaven's sake? She wouldn't employ your services if she didn't know. The irony. All those secrets, and you're employed to find out something that barely qualifies as hidden.'

She flicked some ash towards a nearby ashtray.

'I think it's fair to say you've got what you came for,' she said. It wasn't a question, it was an invitation to leave. Lechasseur accepted it.

Lechasseur was followed from the moment he left Amanda's flat.

Cheap novels and films talk about a sixth sense – the uncanny ability to know you're being watched, followed, or that a man's talking about you. Lechasseur knew more than most about that, but this time his method was more mundane: he could see the two of them.

It was the same men as last night. Did they want him to see them? They certainly weren't making an effort to conceal themselves. Neither were they in any hurry to catch up with him. Lechasseur guessed they were trying to make a point. They knew where he was, they knew they could catch up with him any time they chose to.

They'd revealed something about themselves, though, and it intrigued Lechasseur. They were watching Amanda's flat, not Simon Brown. This worried him. There was a simple explanation for all this, he knew that. They were policemen. They were investigating something. But Simon Brown's role? Amanda's role? Him? There were dozens of possibilities and permutations.

Emily was waiting for him at the café.

It was in the shadow of the British Museum, and was genteel and slightly old-fashioned, full of the clink of china and the hiss of kettles. The waiter led Lechasseur to Emily's table, and she smiled when she saw him. They were the only customers here, but the waiters still managed to find things to do other than take Lechasseur's order. Perhaps they hoped that Lechasseur and Emily could occupy themselves admiring the wood panelling, or the bone china. But he really needed his coffee, the first of the day, and it would be nice to eat some eggs.

The men who'd been following him had melted away; they'd not come into the place after him, but Lechasseur knew they'd be nearby.

Still, this was privacy.

'Did you see him?'

'I recognised him from the photo,' she assured him. 'Not that there's much to recognise. He's so bland.'

'You followed him?' Lechasseur asked.

'Yes. Are you all right?'

Lechasseur realised he'd glanced over at the window. 'Yeah. It's nothing.'

'I followed him. It was easier than I thought it would be. I almost followed him up the steps when he arrived at work.'

'Where?'

'Ministry of Defence.'

Lechasseur nodded. 'I see.' He thought about that for a moment.

'He's a security risk,' Emily suggested.

'Yeah.'

'I don't know what his responsibilities are, but . . . well, he's a black-mail target. He could have all sorts of diplomatic secrets.'

'I think that would be the Foreign Office,' Lechasseur corrected her. 'But you're right about the blackmail. His department would deal with troop strengths and movements. He could work in procurement – that's a big industry, a lot of money at stake.'

Emily was looking at him a little blankly. Some aspects of ordinary life – cooking, driving a car, eating in a café – came naturally to her. Others meant nothing to her. The strangest things – buying a train ticket, tuning a radio, even basic knowledge of the history and politics of the last hundred years.

'What have you been up to?' she asked him.

'I went back to that flat in Bloomsbury. Met Brown's . . . friend.'

'A woman?'

'Of course a woman. Her name's Amanda.'

'And what did you learn?'

Lechasseur wasn't really sure how to answer that. 'Not much,' he concluded. 'They're definitely having an affair.'

Emily, always a little naive, looked disappointed.

'She told me as much,' Lechasseur broke it to her. 'We talked for some time.'

'So who is she?'

'I have no idea,' he admitted.

'You said you talked. What did you talk about?'

Lechasseur struggled to remember. He remembered the long hair, the cigarette holder and its precarious relationship with the cigarette it held. He remembered being offered whisky at ten in the morning.

The waiter came over and took their order.

'The A-bomb,' he said, after he'd gone.

'You were discussing atomic weapons? What on earth did you have to say on the subject?'

Lechasseur would have objected, but it was a fair comment.

'You're an expert?' he asked, raising an eyebrow.

Emily frowned.

'What?' he asked.

'I think . . .' but the voice trailed off. 'I mean, I know the principle of atomic fission, obviously.'

'Obviously,' Lechasseur echoed sarcastically.

'You do,' she insisted.

'They're big bombs, they can destroy whole cities. What else do you need to know?'

'The science behind them . . .'

Lechasseur frowned. 'Yeah, right.' Lechasseur watched her carefully, but she was serious, and thought he was the one who was kidding. Bombs terrified him. Preyed on his mind. But he put that to one side for Emily's sake. 'Perhaps you can help. Amanda said there was a new logic. Those were her words. "A new and terrible logic". Do you know what she meant?'

Emily smiled, a little uncertainly. 'You don't have to treat me like an idiot.'

This was the second conversation with a woman this morning that Lechasseur felt he'd lost control of.

'War is easy, now,' Emily continued. 'Easy and far more destructive. The A-bombs that were dropped on Japan were the first, but they're already far more powerful than that, and they'll get more powerful still.'

'But the logic of war hasn't changed, has it?'

'Yes. Because if everyone has A-bombs, no-one will dare start a war. You mass ten thousand tanks on your border, all your opponent has to do is drop one bomb, and your entire army has gone. So war isn't about mobilising troops and moving armies, it's about being able to drop your bomb.'

'But only the Americans and Russians have them.'

'Really?' she looked shocked at the news.

'You had me going there. How do you know all that, but not know who has the bombs?'

'I – I don't know.'

Their coffee arrived. Emily sipped at hers. 'If the British had the A-bomb, which Ministry would look after it?' she asked.

Lechasseur would have answered if they hadn't heard the shot from outside.

Lechasseur used the door frame as cover, tried to get a good view.

'Come back, sir,' the waiter implored him once again. Emily was behind the waiter, silently agreeing. Their instincts were to get under cover. His was to observe.

'We're safe. I think.'

He tried to get a better view. The two men who'd been following him were behind their car, each hunched behind a tyre, where they got the most protection.

One of them was dead, Lechasseur was shocked to realise. A head shot.

This just didn't happen in London. Even four years after a war, when every man in his twenties had been trained to fire a gun and many had made souvenirs of their service pistols, there just weren't guns around. And people certainly didn't fire them off in the street.

Another shot. This time, Lechasseur was able to see where it came from.

A tall man, broad-shouldered and with a shaven head. He had a revolver, and was firing at another target. Two more men, cast from the same mould as the others. Had they been following him, too?

Not the most pressing question, because the shaven-headed man was in the very next doorway. He had his back to Lechasseur, and his attention was taken with the policemen. Lechasseur wasn't in the line of fire.

'What are you doing?' Lechasseur heard Emily ask from right behind him.

He didn't waste any time with the distraction: she was smart enough to stay out of the way. Nor did he worry about why the man was shooting. There was no good reason to fire a gun in the street, risking the lives of bystanders. Instead, Lechasseur just clamped his hands together and brought both fists down on the shaven-headed man's skull.

The huge man reeled.

So did Lechasseur.

The contact with the man's head . . . he'd seen something. Skies the colour of battleships, vast white pyramids imposed on the London skyline. The smell of old cabbage and diesel.

The blow should have knocked the man out. Hell, it could have killed him. He'd been hurt, but not stopped. Now he turned to face Lechasseur – looking more surprised than hurt – and he'd lashed out at him before Lechasseur had recovered.

The swipe wasn't very well-aimed, but almost took his head off anyway. Lechasseur fell back, stumbling into Emily.

'Get back,' he said, surprised by how weak his voice sounded.

He lurched back at his attacker, punched him square in the face, followed it up with a blow to the stomach, then another.

The man spat defiance at him, thrust out his chin.

Lechasseur brought his head down over the man's nose, breaking it and putting him out for the count.

Emily pulled Lechasseur out of the way as the man dropped to the ground like a felled tree.

The three surviving men were pounding over, stuffing their guns into their jackets.

'Who is he?' Emily asked.

'I don't know.' The man lying on the ground in front of them was huge, wearing a cheap suit. His hair was brown, closely cropped. There was evidence of scarring on the back of his head.

'Does he have the papers?' one of the men asked.

'A wallet?' said one of the others.

The man who had first spoken quickly and efficiently searched through the fallen stranger's clothes, but came up with nothing. He turned on one of his colleagues. 'Empty. Looks like he had the chance to pass them on . . . and *you* were meant to be following him!'

Emily grabbed Lechasseur's arm.

'Where's he from?' she asked.

'I wish I knew,' Lechasseur replied.

And then they were standing in a field, and it was the middle of the night.

CHAPTER 3

It was dark, colder even than an winter's day, practically silent. Most importantly, it wasn't where they had just been. This was the countryside, not London. They were standing in a field. She could just make out the trees; she thought she'd just heard an owl; the ground beneath her was mud, which yielded and sucked at her best shoes.

'Honoré,' Emily whispered.

He was reeling. Disorientated, like she was.

This was a ploughed field. She'd wondered for a second if it was one of the London parks. Leaving aside how they'd got here, or why it was suddenly night, that seemed almost plausible. But they didn't plough up the lawns of the parks; they didn't plant hedgerows. And even in the dead of night, the traffic noise never died away in London. There was always the sound of people, of cars, of trains. The horizon should have been glowing with all the street lights.

Emily was suddenly seized with the idea that this was Hammersmith Bridge, that this was her death. She twisted around, tried to escape it. But there was no river, let alone a bridge.

'Honoré,' she repeated.

He was clutching his head.

'You're dead,' he told her.

'I'm not,' she said, a little redundantly. Then, more firmly. 'No, I'm not.'

'Saw your body,' he growled, as if that settled it.

'I'm talking to you. If I'm dead, how can I talk to you?'

'You're trying to trick me. Blurred vision. Drugged me.'

'Listen, Honoré: if I'm dead, how could I be trying to trick you or drug you?' And why, Emily thought, was she even trying to use logic in this situation?

'Not you.'

'What?'

He shrugged her off his sleeve and stumbled a couple of steps away.

'Where are you going?'

'We were in London.' He said it with such conviction that Emily almost believed him. 'It's the day. I must be in London.'

Emily hesitated and looked around.

'You can see we aren't,' she concluded.

'Shut up!' he called back at her. He was marching away. 'We must be. We must be.'

Her shoes weren't meant for this. She began picking her way after him. Her eyes were getting used to the darkness by now. Her coat was hanging up in the cafe, and it was cold. But it was a spring night, not a winter one. There were buds on the trees.

Which was a little disconcerting, because this was December. Even if they were in the Southern hemisphere, it would be high summer, not Spring. And this was unmistakably the English countryside; there were a hundred little clues that was the case, from the smell of grass in the air to the rows of hedges.

They needed to work out where they were, and they needed to work out why. But she needed Honoré to be a bit more coherent first.

He'd reached the edge of the field. There was some sort of track way. He'd paused there, like it was an impassable stream. There was a rumble; not so much the sound, more the transmission of the sound through the earth.

'You hear that?' he asked.

'What is it?'

They both found themselves some cover as the vehicle approached. It just seemed like the sensible thing to do. It picked its way up the pathway, struggling a little. Emily looked over at Lechasseur, but could barely see him in the poor light. The vehicle didn't have its lights on. The driver either had better eyesight than either of them, or knew his route well.

'Tank,' Lechasseur said under his breath.

'It can't be . . .' But it was a tank, and it came right past them, so close that Emily could have reached out to touch it. It was painted a muddy brown, and clanked and hissed like an old steam train. There were symbols painted crudely on its side. All its hatches were tightly shut.

'Army surplus,' Emily said when it was past them. Lechasseur was still crouched down, checking no more were coming.

'It wasn't there. I could see right through it.'

'What? It was a tank,' she noted. 'Things don't get much more solid than that.'

He'd stepped onto the track, but gingerly, like he wasn't sure where the ground was.

'Honoré?'

He looked scared.

'Calm down?' she suggested.

He shuffled around. 'Is this a road or just a track?'

'Just a track. You were a soldier. What were those symbols? What make was the tank?'

'British,' he said. 'It was a Churchill.'

'It was in a state. What's the expression? "Been through the wars".'

'No. Makes no sense.'

Emily rolled her eyes. 'Which part of this does?'

'You're dead. Be quiet. Confusing me. Ghost tanks . . .'

'Well . . . what do you think is happening?'

'Normandy. I can't still be in Normandy. But . . . what else . . . what . . . ?' the voice trailed away, and she'd not heard him so broken.

'Where you were wounded? Can you see anything?'

'No. I can, but it makes no sense. I'm just as lost seeing like that. Perhaps I'm dead, too?' he suggested.

Emily was a little taken aback. She thought about it for a moment. Bullets had been flying, that man had hit Honoré hard. Perhaps they'd been killed.

'Not a bit of it,' she said. 'This is a place. There's no afterlife. That's all just superstition.'

Lechasseur looked at her properly for the first time. 'It is?'

'Yes,' she told him, with authority.

'Then . . . ?' he left the question hang. 'Why could I see through that tank?'

'I don't know. I couldn't. But you're the time sensitive. It must be something to do with that. We were in London,' she agreed. 'Now we are here. Somehow, we've been moved. We need to find out how.'

'Where are we?'

'We need to find out that as well.'

Lechasseur coughed. 'Anything else?'

'Can you answer either of those first two questions?'

'No.'

'Then any other questions can wait.'

They set off down the path, headed in the opposite direction to the tank. Emily asked Lechasseur to tell her about the vehicle.

Lechasseur looked at her. 'You said other questions can wait.'

'That's the biggest clue we've had. Explain the tank, explain where we are.'

'Russia,' Lechasseur said.

'Russia?'

'When the German army advanced into Russia, they wiped out most of the tank divisions. The British sent tanks in. Arctic convoys. The Soviets drove old British tanks until they got their own factories back working.'

'Were those markings Russian?'

'No. And you can't see through Russian tanks.'

'Oh. But it makes sense – the Russians wouldn't be able to maintain British tanks that well, would they? So that's why it looks dilapidated.'

Emily looked around. She didn't know very much about Russia. But she knew it was a big country. It straddled the world from the ice to the desert, from Europe to China. There must be parts of it with the same climate as England. It was as good a theory as they had.

How they got here was another question.

'Chloroform,' Lechasseur said.

'What do you mean?' she wondered if it was a Russian place name.

'We were knocked out. Flown to Russia. It took hours – that's why it's night.'

Again, this all made sense.

Emily's spirits were lifted at the thought they were making progress. And they'd reached a junction where the path met a wider, tarmac road. She had the real sense they would soon solve this mystery.

Then they found a road sign.

LEEDS 83 KM.

'Perhaps there's a Leeds in . . .' Emily started to say, before stopping herself.

'Fifty-two miles,' Lechasseur said.

'It must be about that,' she agreed.

'The sign . . .'

'It's in kilometres. English road signs are in miles.'

'It's in miles,' he said defiantly. Then, a little less certainly, 'miles and kilometres.'

Emily really couldn't see how to argue her case.

'We should find somewhere safe to sit down and work this out,' she suggested instead.

'Why not here?'

'If there are tanks here, it's not safe. There will be a farm building, something like that, close by. Let's find it.'

It took them less than ten minutes. A barn. Although Emily couldn't work out quite how its roof was staying on. There wasn't a door. It was full of bales of hay, with scraps of rusted farm machinery sitting on a bench laid against one wall.

Honoré was pacing around, reminding her of a drunk. He'd had pretty bad shell shock during the war. Perhaps this was a relapse, brought on by seeing the tank. Although it had started before then, come to think of it.

Emily was grateful to sit down. Her shoes were caked in mud. She tried wiping some of it off with a handful of straw.

'Kilometres,' Lechasseur said.

'Yes,' Emily said, puzzled.

'On an English road sign?'

'We don't know that we're in England.'

Lechasseur was silent. She couldn't see him very well, but knew what he was thinking: of course this is England. He was looking for any certainties.

'We don't know that for a fact,' she reminded him. 'How would we prove it?'

Emily started to look around. She stood and stepped over to the workbench. The pieces of machinery could have been anything, although they looked like engine parts. She moved one chunk aside, and tugged up the scrap of newspaper it had been rested on.

'You think you can use your gift?' Emily wasn't all that clear on how Honoré's ability to see the timelines worked. She wasn't sure he was.

He looked distracted.

'Can you read this?' she asked him, pressing the paper into his hand.

He glanced at it, then passed it back. 'Can you?'

Emily assumed he meant that he couldn't in the darkness, but when she peered at him, she saw the problem. The newspaper was printed in a language that looked more like a telegram than English prose. It didn't seem beyond her, though it would take a little time to decipher. There was a picture of a tank just like the one they'd seen, sat in countryside just like the countryside they were in. She started at the top.

'Honoré. Look at the date.'

2 MARCH 1980

It was an old newspaper. Lechasseur studied it carefully for almost a minute, squinting at it like he needed glasses.

'A woman Prime Minister,' he said, almost laughing. 'An actor standing for President. It's a joke. It's some sort of hoax.'

Emily looked at the paper again. 'Where?' she asked.

'The picture,' he insisted.

'It's a photograph of a tank.'

'No!' As Lechasseur took the paper back, he almost dropped it, as if he'd snatched a branding iron.

'What is it?'

'I can see it. This paper's a few years old. It was brought in here to mop up oil. It was read by a woman and her family. Two sons, her father. It was printed in London. It . . . '

He dropped the newspaper, apologising.

'It was printed in 1980,' he confirmed.

'We're in the future,' Emily said quietly. It explained everything they'd seen. It didn't give them a single clue how they'd ended up here.

'There's a farmhouse near here. Or there was when the paper was brought in here.'

'Fresh hay,' she said. 'Fresh hay and ploughed fields – the farm is still running. If we talk to them, they might be able to help.'

Lechasseur was sat on the floor, clutching his head. 'Stop it!' he shouted.

Emily tried to shush him. It worked, after a fashion. But they weren't going to convince any of the locals of anything if they saw him in this state. She told him to stay where he was while she went to the farmhouse. Lechasseur was grateful, telling her he only wanted some peace so that he could figure things out for himself.

Emily was just as grateful for some peace of her own.

She made her way out of the barn. She wasn't sure, but she thought it was beginning to get light. The sky on the horizon was a deep, rich blue, not the black of night.

It was quiet.

Emily was beginning to doubt her own sanity. Not as much as she was doubting Honoré's, of course, but a rational approach to take was that her mind was far more likely to flip over and go wrong than the entire rest of the universe. She had no memories from more than a few months ago, when she was found on the bombsite; she'd seen her own dead body yesterday; she'd been attacked twice in the street since then. She had to face the possibility that she was suffering some form of shock and so couldn't rely on her perceptions.

Emily decided, instead, to enjoy the sunrise for a moment. It was quite flat countryside, but not completely flat. If this was England, it was the Cotswolds or the Yorkshire Dales, not Cumbria or East Anglia. As the sunlight made its first sorties into the countryside below, Emily was struck by how beautiful it was. And how timeless. Of course, there was evidence of man – the field patterns and the grazing sheep wouldn't be there without agriculture – but this place would look much the same if they'd travelled two hundred years into the past, or two hundred years into the future.

How did she know that? About the future?

She shook her head, trying to dislodge a thought, then realised that there was someone looking at her.

It was a woman in her mid-sixties, possibly older. She was short, dowdy in worn work clothes. Her hair had tinges of red among the grey. Emily didn't like to speculate if it was tinted or not.

'Hello?' Emily said slowly.

The woman looked her up and down, almost confused.

'Those clothes,' she said finally.

Emily wouldn't have stood out from the crowd in London in 1949, and it only now dawned on her that she must have looked quite remarkable.

'You've ruined them shoes,' the woman scowled. 'Nice shoes.'

Her own boots looked worn through.

Emily introduced herself. The woman wasn't interested, and looked minded to turn away and go back to whatever she'd been doing.

'Um . . . is your husband around?' Emily asked.

'Died twelve years back,' she replied.

'Right . . . er . . . your son? Sons?' she said, remembering what Honoré had seen.

'At the front. Both of them.'

Emily found herself craning her neck to look for the front of the building before she realised what the woman was saying.

'The battle front?' Emily asked.

'Ay.'

Emily remembered the newspaper. Honoré had said it was years old, and it looked like it, and there had been a tank on the front of that.

'The war's been going on a long time,' Emily suggested. 'Too long.'

The woman looked at Emily as though her next observation was going to be that the sun came up in the morning or that you got wool from sheep. Emily hesitated before saying anything else. The woman kept standing there, just looking at her, a little suspiciously. She didn't look nervous or angry. Just weary.

'Where are we?' Emily asked.

'My farm.'

'I mean . . . '

'Village is down there,' she said, pointing down the hill. Then she turned away and started trudging off to one of the other outbuildings. Their conversation was over, and Emily was left wondering whether to tell Honoré where she was going. She could see the roofs of the village behind the rise now she'd been pointed towards them. It was five minutes walk at most. Still very early in the morning, but farmers got up early, didn't they? There would be at least some people around.

The village was little more than a dozen limestone cottages, a pub and a shop. The road was pocked with potholes and had crumbled away altogether for one stretch where there was more hole than road.

It was getting light by the time Emily arrived. There was no obvious sign of life: no lights at the windows, or smoke coming up from the chimneys. On the way down, Emily was sure she'd heard a plane. It had been a spluttering engine sound at any rate, possibly a motorbike or small van in the distance.

A side door of the shop was open, and a woman was putting out a bale of newspapers.

'Hello there,' Emily said, trying to sound cheerful.

The woman barely looked up.

'I was looking for, er, some breakfast.'

The woman shuffled aside, and it took Emily a moment to realise she was being invited inside. The shop was dark, and smelt of cabbage. The shelves were almost bare. There were a couple of drab packets of powdered milk, some faded stationery. The windows were shuttered and the only source of light was a television set into the wall, which cast flickering sepia light over the shop, draining any chance of colour from the room. Emily stared into the screen, mesmerised by the pictures of warships ploughing through the sea, firing their cannons at some unseen enemy. Her own face was reflected in the screen. She realised just how much she stood out here, compared with the two local women. She had the merest hint of lipstick, barely a dusting of foundation, but she looked almost impossibly glamorous, like she belonged on the screen, not on the other side, staring in.

'Anything you want here?' the woman said. She was busying herself at the counter.

There wasn't much to choose from. Emily glanced back at the woman, who looked away a little too quickly.

Emily wasn't sure why, but she felt she should leave. She made her way to the door, and found it blocked by a young man in a grey uniform, who was clearly some sort of military policeman.

'Show me your papers,' he said.

'I don't have any . . . any of them with me,' Emily said, acutely aware he'd have noticed the change of story halfway through the sentence.

There had been a minute when the shopkeeper could have telephoned the police, she supposed, but only the barest minute. Had it been the old woman up at the farm who'd tipped the police off?

'Arms up,' he ordered, then moved over, patted her down. He might have been searching for her papers, weapons or something else. But there was nothing there for him to find. He didn't seem to take any pleasure in the procedure, which was something, at least.

'Where are you from?'

Emily wished she knew. 'London,' she answered.

'Why are you dressed like that?'

'It's just the way I dress.'

'Your work?'

She wasn't sure what she was being asked. Did she dress like this because of her work? Did a skirt and a dab of lipstick really mark her out as a whore?

'I do office work,' she told him.

'In London?'

She nodded.

'You're a long way from the office.'

'I'm on holiday.'

He looked at her almost as though he was sorry.

'Come with us.'

It was only then she saw the other four uniformed men outside, behind him.

CHAPTER 4

Emily was put in the back of a rusty van, painted the same grey as their uniforms. It had been the van's engine that she had heard as she was walking down to the village. Three of the men sat in the bench seat at the front, the other two sat opposite her, sorting through the newspapers, checking every page for something.

'These are fine,' one of them said, when they'd studied them all.

'Um . . . what were you doing just then?' Emily asked.

'What did it look like?'

'It looks like you were checking to make sure all the pages were there. But why?'

'It's our duty to recycle,' one of them chuckled. 'Nothing should go to waste.'

Emily wasn't happy with the answer, but their task done, the two men had lapsed into a sullen silence.

Emily couldn't see out of the van, but from the lurching and often slow progress, she got the sense they were travelling along dirt paths as often as they were on proper tarmac. The three men in the front were having some sort of discussion about the quality of the road.

She estimated the journey took twenty minutes. Given all the stopping and starting, she wondered if they couldn't have arrived at their destination faster by walking. She was pulled out of the van by the two men with her. They'd parked – or broken down, she couldn't be sure – on the long, sweeping drive of a manor house. There had clearly once been lawns running here, but they'd all been dug up, and now there were rows of vegetables, with unruly patches of grass here and there. A handful of men and women in overalls were tending to them.

The manor house would never have been beautiful. It was low and the bricks were dark. Over the years it had been extended, and any symmetry there might once had been had broken long ago. Some of the windows had been filled in with ugly cinder blocks. The most remarkable feature, though, was that a great patch of the frontage was covered with posters. Or, rather, many examples of the same small poster of a man in a flat cap with a shovel, surrounded by the words:

DIG FOR VICTORY

One poster on its own would have been lost on such a large house. So another had been placed up next to it, then another. As they'd faded, more posters had been pasted over them, and they'd spread out and up, like ivy. The stark, simple effect of the poster had been completely lost. It made it look as if a part of the house had been constructed from *papier mâché*, or as if it had a scab.

Emily was pushed inside the house. The hallway was small and un-impressive, and had been stripped of its curtains, paintings and carpets.

She was shown upstairs, locked in one of the rooms. Unpainted plaster spotted with damp and bare floorboards.

It was evidently one of the rooms that had had its windows covered up with the posters. The morning light was streaming through the reversed lettering and the fractured, recurring images of the smiling farmer's face and shovel, like grey and red stained glass. It was, in its way, almost beautiful.

The door unlocked after what seemed like moments, and a man in his forties stepped in. The door closed and locked behind him. He was wearing overalls, and it looked like he had hurriedly dressed to get here – his hair looked a little untidy, he hadn't shaved. He carried a tatty cardboard folder.

'Name?' he asked.

'Emily Blandish,' she said.

He noted it on the front of his file, propping it against the wall to write. He had to shake the pen to get it to work.

'You're from London? You work in an office?'

'Er . . . yes.' There had barely been time for the policeman who'd brought her in to compare notes with this man.

He pulled out a photograph and checked it was of her.

Emily blinked, tried to work out when it had been taken. It was the village shop in the background.

'The television was watching me?' she asked.

He looked up from writing something on the back of the photograph, but didn't feel the need to reply.

'No papers?' he asked instead.

'No, like I told the – '

'Your number?'

'My – ?'

He made another note on the back of the photograph.

'You're a long way from London. Explain.'

Emily decided to tell the truth.

'I can't.'

The man sighed.

'I really can't. I was in London, then I was in a field.' She realised she'd edited Honoré out of her story. She hesitated for a moment, but knew she was right to. He was still out there. 'I think I might have lost my memory.'

'You think?'

Emily remembered the intense scrutiny after she'd appeared on the bombsite. The doctors, psychiatrists, journalists. She could make this story stick because it wasn't so very far from the truth.

'Yes. I have amnesia.'

'You know the term?' he asked, throwing her a little until it occurred to her what he must mean.

'With most forms of amnesia, it's the short term memory that's lost. People remember their names, how to speak, all the day to day stuff.'

He watched her closely. 'Quite the expert,' he concluded. 'How do you explain your fancy clothes?'

Emily looked down at her dress. It had seemed rather drab this morning. 'I can't.'

'But you understand why I'm asking?'

Emily smiled. 'Because it's a bit colourful for this year's fashion.'

He looked like she'd sworn at him.

'Who are you?' he demanded.

'Emily Blandish.'

He was looking her up and down. 'Take off your shoe.'

She did as she was told. The mud was drying out, but it was ruined.

'Where did you get this?'

'I told you . . . I don't remember.'

'What do you remember?'

'Waking up in the field.'

'No.'

He seemed so certain, and that threw Emily. 'What?'

'Your dress is clean. If you'd woken up there, you'd have been lying in the mud, it would have covered your dress, like the shoes.'

'I was just standing there. Then I saw the tank.'

'Ours or theirs?'

She frowned. 'Theirs?'

'Was it an enemy tank?'

'I . . . don't remember.'

'You didn't see its markings?'

'It was a British tank,' she remembered. 'A Churchill.'

'You know the make of tank, but you don't recognise which side it's on?'

'Well, unless Britain's being invaded, it's British. Is Britain being invaded?'

'What do you know about that?'

'I told you. I saw a tank. That's all I know about any of this.'

The man took a step back. 'Who are you? You're no foreigner. And you're hardly a spy.'

He didn't wait for an answer, he marched quickly out of the room and bolted the door behind him.

It was about two hours before the door opened again. She was taken out and led into a smaller room, with a concrete floor, bare walls and a television, showing the same newsreel as the one in the shop.

She was soon joined by two men.

The man who'd asked her the questions was followed in by another, broad and shaven-headed. The man who'd been fighting the policemen in London. Instead of a suit, he wore the same grey overalls that seemed to be the style here.

'You!' she cried out, before biting her lip.

'You've met Mr Radford?' the other man asked.

Radford was shaking his head. 'I don't think so.'

The two men circled her like predators, keeping their distance. They looked her up and down.

'What do you see?' the man asked Radford. The way he said *see* made Emily prick up her ears.

Radford reached out, grabbed her by the shoulder. He held it there for a moment, then cupped her chin in his hand.

'I don't . . . ' Radford said, confused.

'Can't see me?' Emily asked, determined to take the initiative.

It worked.

'What do you mean?' the other man asked nervously. 'You know who Radford is? What he can do?'

'I told you,' Emily said. 'We've met.'

Did he really not remember? Radford looked as confused as when she'd said it the first time.

'Simon Brown,' he said. 'She remembers him.'

'I don't recognise the name,' the other man admitted.

'Good,' Radford said.

It had been rather frantic when he'd been firing the gun in the street. Perhaps he'd not seen her, he'd seen only Honoré . . .

'A black man,' Radford said. 'She was in a field with a black man in a leather coat. He was drunk or drugged or . . . I don't know. He is . . . what?'

Emily was struggling to think of something else. Something that wasn't Honoré.

'Lechasseur,' Radford said. 'His name is Honoré Lechasseur. He's . . . '

Radford took a step back, breaking contact with Emily.

'He's like me.'

The other man looked up.

Radford looked thoughtful. 'I want to take her.'

'We want to send her clothes for analysis.'

'She's coming with me. I don't care about her clothes.'

The man nodded. 'There is paperwork.' Then he turned to Emily. 'A change of clothing will be brought. Strip.'

Then he and Radford left her alone to do that.

Emily stripped down to her underwear. By the time she'd done that, a young woman had arrived, carrying a set of grey overalls exactly like her own, a pair of cheap shoes and a paper sack.

She dropped Emily's dress into the sack. 'Underwear and shoes, too,' she said briskly.

She continued to stare at Emily, but there was no curiosity in her eyes.

'Could you turn around?' Emily asked.

The woman frowned. 'Why?'

Instead of arguing, Emily turned so at least she wouldn't have to look at the woman looking at her. When she was done, she saw a ghostly image of herself naked reflected in the glass of the television screen.

Here the televisions watch you.

She put the overalls on very quickly.

Radford's office was on the top floor of the manor house. One wall was sloped, with a couple of grimy skylights. The television here took up the whole of the back wall. Radford sat in front of it, behind a small chipboard desk.

There was nowhere for Emily to sit, so she stood. Her overalls were scratchy against her skin.

Her old clothes were now in neat plastic bags laid out on the desk. One for the dress, one for each shoe, one for her knickers, one for her nylons, one for her watch. There was a seventh bag, which Radford was holding up.

'Where did you get this?'

'What is it?'

He handed it over. It was the scrap of newspaper from the barn. Emily couldn't even remember keeping it, but she must have put it in her dress pocket.

'I found it,' she said.

'It's four years old.'

'So I gather.'

'The Anti-Litter Patrol should have picked it up.'

'The what? Do you mean those men in that van?'

'Newspapers are returned, pulped and recycled. Hoarding newspapers is unpatriotic.'

'It's about three inches square, it's hardly a hoard.'

Radford pulled a rubber speaking-tube from a slot on his desk and gave a quick set of instructions.

A minute later, a small man ran in with a copy of the newspaper, then scurried out.

'The same newspaper, the same date,' Radford told her.

It wasn't the same picture. There was a picture of a tank on the old scrap of newspaper. This one showed a squadron of aircraft on a fly past.

'It must be a different edition,' she said. Newspapers had different regional offices, and different editions throughout the night.

'One edition,' Radford said. 'There is only one newspaper. A man with two watches never knows the correct time.'

Emily shook herself. She knew for a fact she'd only just heard that expression for the first time. She knew she'd said exactly the same thing to Honoré yesterday.

'Sorry?'

'You don't know what to believe, do you? There you have a tank, part of the force that liberated Cairo. Here are our planes, heroically destroying Cairo rather than let it fall to the enemy. If you'd seen only one of these papers, you'd have known what happened. Now you can't be sure.'

Emily looked from one to the other. 'I suppose not.'

Radford was watching her carefully.

'So,' she continued, 'which is true?'

Radford smiled. 'Whichever one I tell you.'

Emily shook her head. 'Either we liberated Cairo or destroyed it. One of these is true, one of them isn't. Regardless of what you say happened.'

'Why does it matter?'

'It matters to the people of Cairo,' Emily countered.

'Does it? Either way, the city was a battleground. Either way, women and children died. They probably saw tanks and planes that day. There was a fierce battle. But ask them who won . . . Why would you take their word for it? Would everyone there say exactly the same thing? And why would it matter to you, anyway?'

'That's what newspapers are for.'

'Yes. To tell you the truth.'

Radford had lit a match. He took Emily's scrap of newspaper from its bag, then set light to one corner, dropping it into an ashtray. It curled and fell apart.

'The planes bombed the city,' he said simply.

He watched Emily for a moment.

'Is that what really happened, or what you want people to believe?'

'Who taught you to think like that?'

Emily frowned. 'No-one. No-one teaches you to think. It's just what people do.'

Radford looked surprised at the statement, and paused for a moment before changing tack.

'Who is the Negro?' he asked. 'Don't lie to me. I saw him clear as day. Honoré Lechasseur. You stick out here, my dear, but around here a giraffe would draw less attention to itself than that man. And he touched that newspaper. So I know he's here. Lying low.'

'How did you know he touched it?'

'Because he's like me.'

'He . . . touched the newspaper.' Emily remembered something. 'He saw a woman prime minister. A photo of one.'

Radford looked like she'd struck him.

'He saw Thatcher?'

'I don't know . . . Is that her name? He didn't say. If you know her name, then . . . wait . . . You said Honoré was like you? You're a time sensitive?'

Radford cocked his head. 'Is that what you call it?'

'It's what someone called him.'

'Describe what you understand by the term.'

Emily tried to collect her thoughts. 'He can see time, like normal people see space. When he meets someone, he can see their past. Most of the time.'

'Then, yes, I am a time sensitive.'

Emily looked him in the eye. 'Then tell me what you see when you look at me.'

'I don't,' he admitted. 'And that's why you're dangerous to me.'

'Dangerous?'

'I have a reputation, Miss Blandish. My ability has allowed me to rise through the ranks of the Party. I am useful, precisely because I am unique, and I am never wrong.'

'And now you are neither?'

Radford's mouth twitched. 'There are three of us in the world. There were five, but two of the enemy assets were targeted and killed. Lechasseur is not one of the other two survivors. So who is he?'

'Don't you have a theory?'

'Not at the moment.' He changed tack. 'You know Simon Brown? You know who he is? His importance?'

'No.'

'Good. Without Simon Brown, this country and its allies would have fallen to the enemy. His role in history was crucial.'

'That man who questioned me first hadn't heard of him,' Emily reminded herself.

'No.'

'If he's so crucial to history . . .'

Radford smiled. 'Why aren't there statues of him in every town centre? Well . . . we don't want people to ask too many questions.'

'But . . . we're . . . at war.'

'What of it?'

'Don't you want to instil a feeling of patriotism? Of nationalism? Make people remember what they are fighting for? The culture, the history?'

Radford laughed. 'No.'

'But . . .'

'That's the last thing we want to happen. It's enough that the people know that they are at war and that the Party is in charge.'

'And Simon Brown comes from a time before that?'

Radford frowned. 'And before that, there was nothing,' he said, with utter conviction. 'The Party has always ruled, there has always been a war.'

'But you know that isn't true.' Emily said.

'Do I?'

'Well . . . you must be at least thirty-five yourself.'

'I'm thirty-seven.'

'Then . . . I know for a fact you were born before the Party took over.'

'You do?'

'Yes.'

'For a fact?'

'Yes.'

'How old are you, Miss Blandish?'

'I'm . . . not sure.'

'You look about twenty-two, twenty-three.'

'I'm a little older, I think.'

'You don't know?'

'I was found on a bombsite.'

'I see. Shell shock?'

'The doctors aren't sure.'

'Would that everyone was like you. Would that we could erase everyone's memories.'

'Instead of collecting up the newspapers every morning, so that no-one can see what you're saying about Cairo now, and compare it with what you said then?'

'Precisely.'

'You thought you'd take Cairo, all the newspapers heralded the great victory, but then Cairo fell to the enemy. So you had to change your story?'

'That isn't important,' Radford insisted. 'The details of the story aren't important. What's important is that it's a story in the first place. Cairo? What happened to Cairo? Who knows? Who cares? Perhaps it fell, perhaps it was destroyed. Perhaps nothing happened in Cairo that day. Perhaps Madrid or Lisbon or Marseilles fell to the enemy, but those cities are all a bit too close to home. Do you remember the headline of that scrap of paper?'

'"Victory!",' Emily told him.

He held up the version he'd been brought.

VICTORY!

'The nature of the victory hardly matters. Every battle ends in victory. That's what the proles notice. They notice the pictures of the tanks or the planes or the smiling Tommy. "Victory!" they think, as they make their way to work. And if that happens, the people who write this have done their job.'

Radford put the paper back down. 'And no-one ever notices that each glorious victory is getting closer and closer to London.'

'That tank I saw . . . was that an enemy tank or one of yours?'

Radford looked at her. 'No memory and you can't tell an enemy tank from a friendly one?'

'No.'

'You may be the perfect citizen. What year were you born?'

'I told you I don't know.'

'You've met Simon Brown.'

'Yes.'

'He died in the first attacks. One of the ironies of history. And that means, if you are telling the truth, one of two things: that you are either far, far older than you look. Or that you're a time traveller.'

'I'm not a – ' Emily began, then stopped.

She was a time traveller.

CHAPTER 5

Lechasseur was getting used to it.

In front of him, a woman in late middle age was handing him a cup of tea.

In front of him, the same woman in late middle age was also handing him a cup of tea.

In one, the woman looked a little less weary. The mug wasn't chipped. He could smell the tea. She was the fainter of the two, almost a ghost.

When you tuned in the wireless, sometimes, especially at night, you'd get the hint of another programme playing. Sometimes it was even in French, or Dutch. There was a simple explanation: they were being broadcast on the same wavelength. Lechasseur would lie in bed listening to it some nights; he often found it quite calming. As if the radio waves were like the ocean waves, navigated by different nations, a great sea that rose and fell around the world.

This was what was happening to him now. But instead of two radio programmes, there were two realities.

Lechasseur couldn't pretend that this was a comforting thought. The idea of two worlds scared him. For a fleeting moment, he'd wondered if there were more than two, but his mind had run from the thought, in case he started to see them all at once.

Instead of multiplying realities, he'd tried to pick one. He'd wondered about the implications of his choice. Would the other one cease to exist, the moment he'd made his decision? Would he be able to change his mind?

He didn't want his mind to change any more, he wanted certainty. And he wasn't God, he wasn't so arrogant to believe that he could create and destroy a planet on a whim. No, he was just a crystal set that needed tuning.

This was the best job he could do for the moment. He'd arrived in the field with neither of the realities taking precedence. Both carried equal weight. A tank had and hadn't trundled past the moment.

Emily had seen the tank, and that was good enough for him.

He picked his universe, and sipped at the tea.

'Thanks,' he said.

The woman looked at him, a glimmer of curiosity in her eye. They obviously didn't get many tourists down this way. She found his accent impenetrable. It was mutual.

He needed to find Emily.

If he caught up with her, he would be able to retune himself to the other reality. He was pretty sure of that.

This woman seemed suspicious of him, but he'd been with her the whole time – she'd not tipped off any family, or the authorities. But he was reluctant to tell her about Emily, in case this exposed her to danger.

'I had two sons,' she told him. 'Both killed. You've been hurt, too.'

'Caught in an explosion in Normandy,' he told her.

She nodded, although he doubted she had any idea where Normandy was.

'You need to settle down,' she told him.

'I do that.' Lechasseur finished his tea and stood. 'Thanks for the tea, but I have to be going now.'

He smiled at the woman and stalked out of her house. Finding Emily was going to be hard. He scanned the countryside and spotted a track leading up to a small wood. If he could get higher up, then maybe he could assess the lie of the land. With a sigh, he headed off up the track, hoping that Emily had not got herself into any more trouble.

After a short walk, he emerged into a clearing. He looked around. Here, he was away from it all: out of sight of the house, the village, any sign of human beings and their wars and other troubles. It was around midday, and he was watching the sun through the trees At the bottom of the hill was a stream, one that would eventually run into the village.

'Hello there.'

Lechasseur looked up and saw the speaker. A woman. He was sure he recognised her. She was in her seventies, with waist-length grey hair.

'Honoré Lechasseur,' she told him. 'The detective. Fancy meeting you here.'

The penny dropped.

'Amanda?'

It was the woman from the flat, twice as old, wearing faded overalls instead of her faded silk gown.

'You remember me?' she seemed flattered.

'Like it was yesterday.'

'I remember you. But why haven't you changed? Aged?'

Lechasseur wondered if he could trust his eyes. There wasn't a ghost image of her. What did that mean?

'Why are you here?' he asked.

She looked around herself. 'I was given instructions . . . many years ago, just after our . . . meeting.'

She lifted an envelope she was carrying. 'I have to deliver these to the house. Over there.'

Lechasseur looked to where she was indicating. A path lead away from the clearing down the hill.

'What's in it?'

'I don't know.'

Lechasseur raised an eyebrow.

'Honestly, I don't know. I was given money, this envelope, and instructions to deliver it here, on this day, by a man called Radford.'

'What did this Radford want in return?'

Amanda looked pained. 'It seemed a fair bargain at the time. A few papers in exchange for wealth and a way out.'

'And the catch was . . .'

'This is all my fault. The atomic war, the rise of the Party . . . this.' She swept her arm around.

Lechasseur didn't have to remember that far back to recall that Amanda was prone to the theatrical gesture, and was more than a little self-centred.

'I doubt it,' he told her, in a tone that he hoped suggested that she get some sense of perspective.

Then she told him.

*

The old world ended on the twenty-first of January 1950.

When Amanda said the world ended, she meant that. It didn't change, it didn't have some new thing or person to cope with, it ended. The old world, the way it worked, it all ended. Politics, economics, history, religion, culture, liberty . . . for a few months they had seemed like luxuries that would need to be rationed for the duration. Then they'd all withered away. Soon they'd all been forgotten. There was only the Party. There had only ever been the Party. Amanda had fled to the country, here to Yorkshire, the home of a friend. It was worst in London, you see, because there, every square inch was –

Lechasseur asked her to start at the beginning. Amanda struggled to. It was as if she was doing that 'tuning' he'd had to do, as if she had to travel mentally to an alien planet, the world of 1949, and London, and silk gowns and history books about trade unions.

She'd met Simon Brown in early July 1949 at some dinner party. He was a civil servant, but a young one. He'd returned from the War determined to rebuild the world, to see that great things came from the horror and death he'd witnessed in the Far East, the murder and destruction that had consumed virtually the whole world.

Amanda's husband had died during the War, left her everything, and she'd sold it all and moved to the biggest place she could afford in Bloomsbury. She'd spent much of the War reading, and knew that the country would be different when the fighting ended. If nothing else, women were used to working, and there would be fewer men around. The traditional family was a thing of the past.

Simon was married, with a young child.

That night at the party – Amanda paused at the word: she'd forgotten that 'party' had once meant something quite different – she'd told him her theories. He was ten years younger than she was, and had lapped up her every word like it was the gospel truth. He'd known nothing of the Left, of the rise of Communism, of the workers' struggle, of the inevitability that this old order would be swept away.

She'd led him up to a guest room and undressed. She'd told him that much Socialist thought depended on free love and the abandonment of bourgeois notions of monogamy, which was simply a method of social control. Their act was a political one, not merely a physical one. She'd neglected to mention that she'd been lonely since the death of her husband, that it felt good for a younger man to stare at her, kiss her, to paw at her, to hold her down.

Lechasseur suggested that she didn't need to tell him everything.

The relationship had continued, she told him. He'd meet up at her flat. They'd talk in bed, swap history books and the occasional novel or magazine article. It had been a whole six weeks before the subject of atomic weapons had come up.

Simon Brown had done a degree in Physics at Cambridge, and one of his jobs was to translate some technical papers into a form that his more Classically trained superiors could better understand. He'd proved adept at this, and was seeing more and more papers. There was some system in place to prevent him seeing every secret document, but the more papers he saw, the more he could piece together. Holidays and absences meant that he often saw many more papers than he strictly should have done.

Before long, he'd become probably the only man in England who knew the exact state of the British atomic weapons programme. He'd suspected it was some sort of loyalty test, an entrapment exercise, and he'd been scrupulous in keeping the secrets. Soon, though, it'd became abundantly clear that he was giving his political masters more credit than they deserved. They didn't understand that they were handing him an almost complete picture of the field.

Amanda hadn't known any of that when she'd told him the latest thinking about atomic weapons. Philosophers and thinkers had realised that it revolutionised war, turned it on its head because –

Lechasseur stopped her. He'd had this conversation with Emily.

Amanda had explained to Simon that she thought that the only way to prevent the atomic bomb from being the ultimate tool of imperialist oppression was if it could be made to act as a deterrent.

Lechasseur stopped her again. That's what had been happening, surely?

The Americans had beaten the Japs by threatening to use the bomb, not by wiping them out. And now, the one thing stopping Joe Stalin from sending the Red Army into Europe was the threat that they'd be wiped out in an atomic holocaust. What had happened in Berlin since last summer . . . or thirty-six summers past . . . would have led to war in any earlier age. Instead, the city divided, there was peace. Uneasy peace, but better than war.

A long-forgotten memory flickered across Amanda's face. That wasn't true deterrent. That was people being scared of America. And the United Kingdom – she said the words carefully, as if pronouncing Latin – wanted their own atom bomb for the same reason. It was an ally of the United States, but that might not always be the case. Far more likely, Simon told her, that in a situation involving purely British interests, America might not be willing to bomb our enemies. Atomic deterrent only worked if your enemy knew for certain that the bomb would drop.

Simon knew what only a few men in the world knew: there were just a handful of atom bombs. The materials involved were so rare, there were so few entrusted with the secrets. In 1949, the Americans had a mere handful of bombs, and each bomber had a one in ten chance of reaching a city deep in the Soviet Union. They couldn't know for certain that even one atom bomb could hit its target.

She laughed as she remembered that their foreplay consisted of her telling him the latest political thinking. How Stalin wasn't worried about the bomb, but the Americans were thinking of pressing ahead now, while they had the advantage. It aroused them both; they liked to imagine themselves great minds, they liked to link what they were doing to the great struggle of the workers. She found that comical, now, that her reciting Marx or Engels or even just Wells at him as he cupped her and licked at her and trailed his finger over her was anything other than exactly the sort of middle-class decadence they both despised.

Amanda had been telling him about a pamphlet she'd been reading on atomic warfare. She had said that if every country had the bomb, then no-one would ever dare start a war. No-one would mass an army on a border, or switch a whole industrial area to munitions production, or assemble a naval taskforce. War would end, but only if every country had the bomb.

Simon had stopped cold.

'I could do that,' he had told her.

Simon was confused at first – surely the bomb was evil? Surely it was the weapon of plutocrats and dictators? Finally, one man could wipe out a million workers, as so many robber barons and union busters and corporation chairmen had wished they could.

Only while it remained in the hands of a few, Amanda insisted, seeing Simon in a new light, suddenly. She realised she shared a bed with the most powerful man in the world – the only human being to combine political enlightenment with the ability to enact it. It excited her, and Simon Brown forgot all about politics for a moment.

As he took her, though, and as she screamed his name, Amanda's mind was elsewhere.

'You sold atom secrets to the Russians?' Lechasseur said, full of contempt for this stupid old woman.

'No. They had them already. They knew everything that Whitehall knew. But Stalin . . . none of us really thought he was perfect. You mentioned Berlin. Well, you probably remember the blockade better than I do. He was another Hitler. Exactly the sort of dictator our plan would neutralise.'

'Then?'

'We gave the world the bomb,' Amanda explained. 'The papers I sold . . . they were circulated widely throughout the scientific and literary communities. It spread faster than the plague, copies being copied and passed on and copied and passed on. Soon, every thinking man could build an atom bomb.'

'You just said that they use rare materials. That not even America had that many.'

'True.'

'So, in less than a year, you're saying there were enough bombs around to . . .'

'No-one ever built one of our bombs.'

'What?'

'Don't you see? No-one had time to. It would take months or years to build an atom bomb, even with a team of scientists and all the materials you needed.'

'Then?'

Amanda had a tear in her eye. 'The men who had the bombs already wanted to maintain their monopoly. That's how they'd always worked. In the West, it was the men who owned the railways, or the merchant fleets, or the oil, or the automobile factories, or the mines, or the steelworks. A tiny number of rich men, controlling the economy. In the East, it was the same. A handful of men with political and military power. Capitalist or Communist, it didn't matter. What mattered was that power was concentrated in the hands of a few.'

'But if everyone had the knowledge . . . you can't just lock up everyone.' Amanda sighed.

'That's precisely what they did. Knowledge is power, and we'd given everyone the ultimate knowledge, the ultimate power. And before it could be used, it was taken away. The libraries burned, the universities were closed, every newspaper and publisher was taken over. They piled every book onto bonfires, and when that didn't work, they rounded up every scientist, their families, their friends and threw them onto the fires, too. We always used to say that you couldn't uninvent the bomb, but that's exactly what they did. I'd opened Pandora's box, Mr Lechasseur. What came out destroyed the world, and when all that was left in there was Hope, the Party went in, dragged her out and had her shot.'

It was the middle of the morning, and Emily and Radford were walking through the grounds.

Emily was becoming used to the overalls. She'd asked for something to neaten up fingernails that she'd variously bitten or caught on things. Radford had looked at her at first as though she'd demanded to bathe in asses' milk, but had managed to procure a nail file. As she'd taken it, he'd watched her warily, as though she could turn it into a weapon. He was over a foot taller than she, and possibly weighed three times as much, all of the difference being muscle. Her potential as a threat to him was limited, at best.

Now they walked. It was almost pleasant. The sky was clear, a rich, uniform blue. All around them, birds were bobbing in and out of the trees. Emily was warm and no longer thought she was in immediate danger. There were no televisions watching her here, no eavesdroppers.

'But you must see the difference,' she continued.

'There isn't one.'

'Of course there is. History is what happened.'

'It's what someone said happened.'

Emily rolled her eyes. They were going around in circles. 'Technically, but – '

'You have no idea what it is like to be able to have this debate,' Radford told her. 'To have to explain something so obvious to someone so intelligent, it's exhilarating.'

Emily looked over at him. Radford was grinning.

'I'm not sure if I've just been insulted . . .'

'Not at all. No-one thinks like you. So few people even think. Most people would have only the vaguest sense of what you mean when you say "history". To distinguish between the events and the telling . . .'

'This is nonsense,' Emily countered. 'Whatever you want to call it . . . whether it's "history" or "events". Call it "events". Those *events* happened.'

'Not if the Party says they didn't.'

'That's silly. I was there. I was in 1949. I know the world hasn't always been like this. I know that . . . a hundred years ago, that truck wouldn't have existed, we used horses and carts.'

Radford looked puzzled.

'So the truck is a new invention,' Emily explained. 'Things are getting discovered all the time.'

'People don't know that,' he said simply.

'But that doesn't stop it from being true.'

Emily looked around for inspiration. Behind her was the manor house.

'That house. It's obviously old, it self-evidently wasn't built to be your headquarters. There are stables, for a start. And these were obviously once lawns, not vegetable patches.'

Radford conceded the point.

'So it doesn't matter if the people don't know the word "Victorian" or know that this place must be about a hundred years old, they can see that it's been here a long time. Just looking at it, you can see it's been extended and altered over the years.'

Radford was looking back. 'You can tell all that by looking?'

'Even if I couldn't . . . well, if that gift you have is anything like Honoré's, then you must have been able to see that for yourself. You must have seen its history with your own eyes. And whatever the Party tell you, you can see what they are telling you is all lies.'

Radford winced. 'A contradiction in terms. Look . . . who's to say that *events* are more important or more real than *history*? Reality is what we say it is. You're called Emily because we agree that's what you're called. A dollar is worth a dollar because we agree it. It's midday because we say so. We're fighting a war because we say we are. We won a great victory in Cairo. The Party has always ruled.'

Emily smiled.

Radford looked at her. 'What?'

'I saw you before. You were worried about a tiny scrap of newspaper. And you were right to be. Because it doesn't take much. It only takes someone's watch to be a little slow.'

'What?'

'Tell me the time.'

Radford checked. 'It's exactly twelve hundred.'

'You took my watch away. But I bet it doesn't tell exactly the same time as yours. And if my watch tells me it's five to midday, it's five to midday. It doesn't matter what time you say it is.'

They stood there for what seemed like forever. The silence broke as bells started chiming twelve.

'I guess it wasn't exactly twelve hundred,' Emily smiled.

Radford was watching her the same way he'd watched her when she'd first picked up the nail file.

She looked him in the eye, and said: 'If the Party's so powerful, why do they have to keep erasing the past? What scares them so much?'

There was one universe. It had a clear blue sky, with tree branches as thick as jailhouse bars obscuring it. Amanda was there, every line and wrinkle of her face etched on with a clarity that made Lechasseur wonder if they hurt her.

Here, there had been purges, there had been war, there had even, irony of ironies, been atomic bombardment. It worked as deterrent only in times of peace. In war, the use of the bomb became inevitable; all too easy to justify as saving time and lives.

Lechasseur saw it all now. Thirty five years of history unfurled around Amanda, all fitting together like a pocket watch, the ticking of the clock giving way to the march of jackboots and the ratta-tat-tat of machine guns.

Time, he saw now, was a monolith. The universe is what it is, we are where we are, what's done is done, not even God can change the past, so it is written. It didn't matter that he was meant to be on page 1949 but he'd skipped a chapter. It didn't matter how he'd got here or if he got back.

He saw it all as he and Amanda hugged each other, both of them sobbing, perhaps the last two people on Earth to remember the world that had been lost.

London, glorious, filthy, broken London. So full of colour, so full of history. The British Museum had been razed to the ground, its curators machine-gunned in the courtyard. There had been wave after wave of purges and pogroms, broadcast live to every home in loving detail over and over until it seemed normal. Until it was normal.

An image.

Amanda staring at a picture on a school trip. A naked man and a woman stumbling through a blasted wasteland. In the far distance, a splash of green. Above them, an angel with wings and skin of gold and fire, holding a sword. The Archangel Michael, the guide was telling her.

The guide would be long dead. The painting would have been torn down, slashed and broken.

Lechasseur broke away, pulled back.

'I have to find Emily,' he told Amanda.

'You didn't answer my question.'

'Which question?'

'Why do you look the same?'

Lechasseur hesitated. He wasn't entirely sure of the answer himself, but it had something to do with Emily. He had to find her, because with her they might just be able to stop this.

'I think,' he began. 'It's because . . . '

Amanda smiled. 'It's all right. You have to go and find your friend.'

Lechasseur checked his watch. It was five to noon.

CHAPTER 6

'You recognised me,' Radford reminded Emily.

Emily had been dreading that.

'Yes,' she said quietly.

'How?'

'I was mistaken. You reminded me of someone I know.'

Radford shook his head. 'I've never been mistaken for anyone in my life, Blandish.'

She looked up at him, saw him grinning a rather crooked grin.

He reached out, brushed her forehead quite gently.

'1949,' he said. 'You saw me in 1949.'

'Yes,' she admitted.

He considered this information for a moment or two. 'I wonder how.'

'I don't know,' Emily told him, summoning up her courage.

'I'll worry about that, you don't have to,' he told her.

They walked a little further, in silence. Where would she run to, Emily wondered. She wasn't sure where the village was. Over the next hill or ten miles away? She'd asked Radford the time because she'd had no idea how long it had been since she'd left Honoré in the barn. It had been six or seven hours. There was no way Honoré would still be there. He'd have no idea where she was. He wouldn't even know where he was himself, and if he was still in the state he'd been in, then his situation would almost certainly be hopeless.

Her best hope was that he'd be arrested and brought here. But she knew that there was no way Radford would let the two of them meet.

Was that the reason for the walk in the woods? Was Honoré being brought to the manor house for interrogation, and she was being kept out of the way?

She dismissed the idea. Radford would want to question Lechasseur himself.

Lechasseur saw Emily.

He couldn't believe it at first. Amanda had told him about the manor house, and he'd headed up here. But he couldn't have hoped that Emily would be out here, walking around. She was wearing overalls.

The man from London was there. He looked even larger than before.

He and Emily seemed to be deep in conversation. He didn't look like he was armed. They didn't seem to be arguing. She wasn't handcuffed or otherwise restrained. She was just taking a walk with the man, wearing the same uniform as him.

Lechasseur didn't know where Emily was from, how she'd come to be in 1949. Was she from the future? Was she back at home? She looked comfortable here, talking to this man.

He remembered the lined faces of the farmer's wife and of Amanda. He saw the drab overalls. Everything here was worn down, rusted, faded, corrupted. Everything but Emily.

There was a chance he could survive here, fit in, even serve the Party. In his time, he liked to think he walked the line between the legal and the illegal. Here, where nothing was permitted except by the will of the Party, the obvious way to thrive was to be in the Party. But there were shortages here, so whatever the Party said, there would be people who'd make it worth his while to supply them with whatever it was they needed. He could help them, he was sure of that, if that was his fate.

They'd walked a little further. Emily was in two minds: unsure whether to make a run for it, or continue with the conversation. When she found herself thinking that if she ran and was shot, at least it would be quick, she realised that she was panicking. She wasn't, as far as she could tell, in immediate danger. Running, she would be. She didn't think Radford was carrying a gun, but wouldn't like to rule out the possibility.

Radford was looking at her. Could he sense what she was thinking?

'So much brightness,' he said.

'Brightness?' Emily frowned.

'You. You think. You question. It's unusual. It's – '

He leant in and kissed her, rather roughly. A moment later, his hand was pushing its way into her overalls, rummaging for her breast.

Emily pulled back, pushed her way out of his arms.

'What the hell do you think you're doing?' she shouted at him. 'What the hell?'

She stumbled away from him, terrified.

Radford was coming after her.

Her immediate instinct was to run. She moved away, already realising that she didn't have anywhere to go, and that he would catch up with her within a few paces, that he could have been carrying that gun.

He was following, she could feel his feet pounding into the ground behind her.

Radford grabbed her shoulder, then she felt him relent, and let her go.

'I don't know . . .' he started to say.

'Why? Did you think I . . . I didn't want you to . . .'

Radford stood tall, remembered who he was. 'You're my prisoner, and – '

'So you want to pay me a compliment, then grope me?'

'You will stand still.'

'I am standing still. You explain why you did that.'

Radford looked at her for a moment. 'I can't. I'm sorry . . . it's been so long. If I could go back and stop myself from – '

Emily didn't have time to flinch as he touched her shoulder.

Lechasseur saw it with his own eyes, for a moment at least.

They'd been walking together, she'd been smiling, laughing even. Then the man – the same man who'd been killing men on a London street – kissed Emily, slid his hand into her clothing. They thought they were alone. Away from the cameras and the microphones.

Lechasseur turned away, started walking in the other direction. They didn't want him to see what happened next, and he didn't have any desire to see it. He kept his head down.

Lying on a stainless steel table in a police morgue.

He wanted to protect Emily, but she was going to die. History was written, and it couldn't be unwritten. Lechasseur didn't understand why he was so angry. It wasn't jealousy, he knew that much. He just didn't think of Emily that way.

It was frustration, he decided. This morning, life had been okay, London was rebuilding, and he was doing all right for himself. Now he knew the future, and was condemned to return to 1949 to live it out. It was like getting on a train he knew would crash. Not just a warning or a feeling. It wasn't a risk, it was a certainty.

Emily would die. Whatever she and that man were doing now. However he was making her feel.

The shock of seeing her naked body.

She'd soon be dead. The man would break her neck and leave her lying in the mud.

Lechasseur reeled.

The man with the shaved head. He was the murderer.

He *saw* it now.

The man standing there, boots heavy with mud. Emily dropping to the ground, her body unable to support itself as there was no life, no instinct left. The man stood over her for a moment, utterly without emotion. Killing her had no moral or legal implications. It was just necessary.

He would kill her, it had already been written.

Lechasseur pitched round, started back towards Emily and the man. Whatever they were doing now, whatever she was consenting to, he had to get Emily away from here. He found himself running, but . . .

Emily wasn't there. The man she'd been with was gone, too.

This was impossible. Just a few moments ago, they'd been here. Lechasseur had already passed the point he'd seen them. He whirled around, looking for them in the undergrowth, but – apart from the barely-a-path he was on – this was all nettles and brambles. If they were here, he'd have heard them, and they would have heard him.

Even if they'd broken into a gallop the second he'd turned his back on them (and the reason he'd turned his back on them was that they weren't about to do that), then he'd still be able to see them.

He suppressed the urge to call out her name.

Somehow, Emily was gone.

He tried seeing her.

She was here, the man's hand on her shoulder. She was behind him, walking into the woods. She was both. She was somehow both.

Lechasseur reeled, like he'd been given an electric shock.

She was both.

Somehow, Emily and Radford were back on the outskirts of the wood.

He was removing his hand from her shoulder. Turning to look at him, she saw the manor house.

The two of them were unsure where to look.

'We . . .' she began.

Radford was pacing around. 'What happened?' he asked her.

Emily stared into the woods. The absurd thought had crossed her mind that she'd somehow see herself in there.

They'd been here just five minutes before.

'I don't know,' she said, replying to Radford. 'Can you see anything?'

For a moment, Radford was clearly trying. Then he stumbled, dizzy.

Exactly the same thing as had happened to Honoré, Emily thought. The last time she'd been one place one minute, another the next.

They stood there for what seemed like forever. The silence broke as bells started chiming twelve.

Emily and Radford looked at each other. He clearly thought it was some kind of trick she was pulling on him. She, for her part, hadn't got a theory.

'Come with me,' Radford ordered.

Emily had little choice but to obey. They headed back to the house, and she was led back up to her cell.

As the bells chimed twelve, Lechasseur picked one – the Emily nearest him, the one who had walked into the woods with her murderer.

He ran towards them, but neither saw him. Instead, the man was reaching out for her. She was trying to get away.

As the man touched Emily's shoulder, and Lechasseur ran straight for him, hoping to knock him off balance, he suddenly wasn't there. Lechasseur found himself running through thin air. Emily had gone, too. If he hadn't been so alert, he'd have crashed into a tree or stumbled into the undergrowth. As it was, he just found himself standing there.

He couldn't rely on his eyes here. He should have known that already.

He'd already seen there was another Emily. He broke into a run, heading towards her, heading to save her life.

On the other side of the wood was a manor house. Emily and the large man weren't here, either, but he hadn't seen them disappear.

Lechasseur began heading towards the house.

She was in there. He had some sense that Emily was in there. If he'd stopped to think, he might have decided it was wishful thinking that she was in the manor house. At best it was a wild assumption.

Two men were coming up to him. One was middle-aged, the other looked like the first's son – the lad was probably just fourteen. So Lechasseur made sure to knock his dad down first, kicking him in the back just in case he was thinking of getting back up. The lad ran off. Lechasseur was pleased about that, because he really wouldn't have enjoyed hitting him.

The front door wasn't locked. It didn't even seem to have a lock. But as Lechasseur reached for the handle, the boy was already heading back, three labourers following him. One of them carried a spade, and this was the one that made the first move.

Lechasseur dodged it, kicked him in the stomach, wrenched the spade out of his hands and brought it down on his shoulder, probably breaking the collarbone.

The other two charged him at the same time. Lechasseur had the spade up, and couldn't get any momentum behind it before they arrived and grabbed at him. He dropped the spade so he could grip at the attackers instead. They were both strong, and Lechasseur found himself struggling to break their grip.

Another man was running up the path. This one had a rifle. As he brought it to bear on Lechasseur from about fifteen feet away, the two men holding him relaxed their grip and stepped aside.

The door to the manor house opened, and the large man, the one who was going to murder Emily, stepped out.

The man stared at him, studied him.

'Where's Emily?' Lechasseur asked.

'You must be Lechasseur.'

'Where is she?'

Two more guards, both with rifles, were trotting out of the house and taking positions by Lechasseur. The man whom Lechasseur had knocked down first was struggling back to his feet.

'Don't kill him,' the large man said quietly.

The guard nearest Lechasseur obliged, knocking him out with the butt of his rifle instead, on the second attempt.

'What's your name?' Emily asked the girl.

She looked up, with dull eyes. She wasn't naturally stupid. When Emily had been found on the bombsite, and the doctors had studied her, some had said she was stupid. No, they'd not used that word. They'd said 'slow' or 'simple'.

'What's the capital of France?' they'd asked. She hadn't known.

'What's the name of the Prime Minister?'

'What's the name of your street?'

'What's your birthday?'

Emily hadn't been able to answer many of their questions. When they'd shown her a picture of a cat, she'd correctly identified it. She knew what a tree was – in fact, when they'd shown her a picture of a tree, she'd said 'Oak', so she'd discovered she knew the names of lots of trees. Her knowledge was there, but it was patchy, inconsistent. There was no pattern to what she remembered and what she didn't – if there was, at any rate, no-one could decipher it.

One doctor had been particularly rude. 'If you don't have a memory, you don't have a personality, you don't have an identity. You're nothing, barely better than a monkey. No more intelligence than a chimpanzee.'

She'd asked him if he had a good memory. He'd told her he did.

'What's the capital of France?' she'd asked.

'Paris,' he'd said, impatiently.

'And you've always known that?'

'I learned it. And remembered it.'

'When did you learn it?' Emily asked.

He'd hesitated. 'A long time ago. I must have been four or five.'

'But you don't remember? You can remember some things, but not others.'

He hadn't accepted the point, so she'd pointed out that a chimpanzee was an ape, not a monkey.

She knew that this girl was uneducated, not stupid. But what angered Emily was that she didn't seem aware she could change that.

The girl had brought her some food, and had obviously been ordered to stay and watch her eat it. This, in itself, intrigued Emily. The meal was cold tomato soup, served in a bowl with a little tin spoon. Was there really some sequence of events that Emily could set off that involved these items and that would lead to her escaping?

Emily struggled to think of a plan. The spoon was so flimsy that she was pleasantly surprised it survived contact with the soup. She could break the bowl and use the shards, she supposed.

Emily was vaguely insulted by having this dull young woman guard her. Some faceless administrator had decided Emily was enough of a threat to warrant a guard, but not enough to deserve a real one.

There was shouting from outside. The girl didn't so much as react, Emily had already set aside her soup bowl, and was at the window, trying to peek out between gaps between the posters pasted to it. But she couldn't see anything.

The girl was tidying away the bowl.

'I've not finished with that,' she told her.

'You put it down,' was the riposte.

Emily tried to be sympathetic. This girl was like this only because she didn't know any better. What was the point of learning anything, in a world where the government lied to you and said only what they wanted you to hear? What did they teach them in schools? Science, history, literature, religion? None of that would be of any use here. Mathematics? A little abstract if all you need to know for your job is how to serve tomato soup. Stupidity was probably a rather good survival option here.

Radford watched Lechasseur.

They'd strapped the prisoner to a chair in one of the Conversation Rooms, but – at Radford's instruction – hadn't administered any drugs.

'Emily has told me all about you,' Radford said, as his opening gambit.

Lechasseur looked up suspiciously. 'She's still alive, then.'

Radford smiled. 'Of course.'

'You kissed her, started to undress her. I saw it with my own eyes. I don't care what you did after that. It's what you're going to do. You're going to kill her,' Lechasseur stated.

'No.'

'I've seen it happen.'

Radford reached out, brushed Lechasseur's cheek, *saw* him.

It was like plunging into an ocean. So much to take in. Normandy. A flash of light, then darkness. Pain. Radford tried to focus. London. Disorientation as he saw someone who looked just like himself, only to realise that it was him. A woman with long hair offering Lechasseur a whisky, Lechasseur seemingly oblivious to the fact she was also offering herself. Emily Blandish, laid out in a hospital room, or a morgue. Marks on her bare neck and shoulder.

Radford became aware that Lechasseur was *seeing* him, *slumped on the pavement, with Emily asking him a question,* and he broke off contact.

Lechasseur smiled up at him. 'Emily's three doors down from here. You tried to kiss her, but she fought you off.'

He should have anticipated this. Radford scowled at himself.

'I've never been to 1949,' he said instead. 'Yet there I am.'

'I can't help you,' Lechasseur said. 'I have no idea how we got here.'

Radford found himself grinning. 'You've already told me quite enough.'

'You don't know, either,' Lechasseur said. 'I'd have seen it.'

'I've only just worked it out,' Radford told him. 'But I'm sure I have it, now. We'll find out, soon enough.'

Lechasseur looked confused.

'I don't need you any more. I'll let Ned and his son ask you a few questions. Remember Ned? You nearly broke his back just now? I'm sure they'll remind you.'

CHAPTER 7

Radford sat behind his desk. Two of the boffins he'd called over from the airstrip were thinking the problem over.

'So, this Emily has some sort of ability? And this isn't the same as the trick you and the Negro can do?' This was the fat one, the radio expert.

'No. Her mind is different.'

'Different?' The thin one was more practical. He designed new aircraft, or at least he adapted the existing ones.

'Yes, just talking to her – she's highly intelligent, she learns fast. But I think there's something more important than that. She's got an instinct. Lechasseur was confused when he arrived. I think he barely believes it now. He copes, he adapts, but it's bloody-mindedness. He doesn't understand.'

'This Blandish woman does?'

Radford nodded.

'She can will herself to different time periods?'

'Not on her own. There needs to be two of us.'

The fat one paused to consider this. 'One of you is the machine, the other is the battery?'

The thin one shook his head. 'No . . . it's more that he's the navigator, she's the pilot. I don't understand Radford's abilities. None of us does. But it's like that. No point flying if you don't know where you're going. He can navigate.'

'I already have,' Radford confirmed.

The two men looked up at him.

'You've time travelled?'

'Five minutes and fifty metres.'

'How?'

Radford grinned at them. 'I touched her, and we both thought about being somewhere else. And we were there. And that's how he and she ended up here. They saw me and she touched him, and one of them said they'd like to know where I came from. Then they were here. They were a hundred metres out, at most. But Lechasseur could trace me across time and space. And I will travel in time again. They've seen me. It's already happened.'

The fat man held up his hand. 'Wait, wait. What do you mean it's happened?'

Radford explained what he'd seen.

'Pity you have to kill her,' the fat one said.

'It's what happens,' Radford said, without regret.

The thin man was smiling to himself.

'Share,' Radford warned.

The thin man looked nervous for a moment, then collected his thoughts. 'You don't have to worry about that,' he said. 'It's a loop in time. You could kill this Emily, then find the other one, the one who's already in 1949. Then bring her here, a moment before you left. Then you'd have two Emilys.'

Radford held up his hand. 'Wait . . .'

The fat man was warming to the theme. 'This is good.'

'How can there be two Emilys?'

'You wouldn't need to take the original one back any more.'

Radford thought about this. 'Wait . . .'

'Think of it this way. When you go back to 1949, what happens?'

'I don't know yet. I arrive. It seems I kill Emily, then I don't know what else I'm meant to do.'

'Lechasseur sneaks up behind you and knocks you out. At the very least – he may even have killed you.'

'Yes.'

'But don't you see? He can't. Not now. Even if you're happy to play your part in history and meekly let him hit you, you can't possibly be surprised when that happens.'

Radford had seen what Lechasseur had seen. Surprise. 'It must be more complicated than that. If I don't take her back, how could I have gone back to get the other one? There are other things – what if I went back and killed my father before he met my mother? I wouldn't be born, so I wouldn't be able to go back.'

'Doublethink,' the fat man said, simply. And that was that. Of course it was. Simply hold the two ideas in your head simultaneously.

'Doublegirl,' the thin man laughed. 'Perhaps if you were to have children, they would combine the two talents.'

The fat one nodded. 'Certainly worth a try.'

Radford wasn't prepared to move on to that just yet, attractive though the proposition was.

'We can rewrite the past,' Radford said.

'We can rewrite any part of it we like,' the fat man said. 'Then, if we don't like it, we can rewrite it again.'

Radford glanced down at the ashtray, and the fragments of charred newspaper.

'Kill our enemies before they are a threat.'

'Pass on information to forewarn our armies.'

'Can you take anyone else with you?' the thin man asked.

Radford shook his head. 'I don't think so.'

'Shame – you could have led a platoon anywhere in history.'

'You can wear things,' the fat man said, glancing at the mud-encrusted shoes bagged on Radford's desk. 'You could carry weapons.'

'An atomic weapon,' the thin man suggested.

'You could deliver an atomic weapon anywhere on Earth, to any point in history.'

Radford gasped. '1949.'

The two men looked over the desk at him.

'Have either of you gentlemen heard of Simon Brown? No, I thought not. Gentlemen . . . I'm going to tell you something I've never told anyone. In my dreams I see another world. No . . . that's not quite true. I see this world, but with a different history. Always the same history. There's no Party there.'

The two men made worried glances at the screen.

'This is just your dream? What do you see?'

'I travel the world and the seven seas. Everybody's looking for something.'

'Pardon?' the thin man asked finally.

'Something from that other history. A song. The world is very different. Sometimes – ' and now it was Radford's turn to look at the screen ' – sometimes I wonder if that world is how it was meant to be. How it should be: the Apple Macintosh, the Olympics in Los Angeles, the – '

The two men were shuffling their feet.

'We owe everything to the Party.'

'A world without the Party is unthinkable.' The fat man looked concerned saying that – to even have to voice something so self-evident was tantamount to treason. All red apples are red. It never needed iterating.

Radford nodded. 'I agree. But I think we might need to convince history of this. Lechasseur and Emily were investigating Simon Brown. It was a critical time – a word in a different place, a slightly different decision, slightly different timing, and events would be so very different. This can't be a coincidence. This is destiny – a black circle drawn around a moment, with an arrow pointing at it.'

'Scheduled for revision.'

'Exactly. We need to plan this carefully. We need to shut down that other version of history entirely. At the moment . . . at the moment, there are two sets of events. We must eliminate one of them. He who controls the past commands the future. We have the power here to conquer the past.'

The two scientists looked at each other.

'We already control the past . . .'

'Not enough,' Radford countered. 'Not enough. We control history. But by this method, we control the events, not just the telling of them.'

'There's no practical difference.'

Radford shook his head. 'There is.' He paused, grinned crookedly, in a manner that disconcerted the two scientists. 'There was,' he corrected himself.

Emily was making a game of it.

The soup had been cold when it came in, and so it would be no more unpalatable in an hour. So she took her time. Emily glanced occasionally at her watch, and about forty minutes passed before the girl began to get a little uncomfortable. Emily smiled at her, pretended to be cheerful – a process that, itself, made her feel happier – and would occasionally say something upbeat. The girl said nothing at all, and seemed disconcerted.

Once every five minutes or so, Emily would take a spoonful or two of the soup.

The game continued for two hours. The girl was beginning to shift around a bit. Emily suspected she needed the lavatory. But it wasn't difficult to see that the girl had been given very specific orders: serve Emily soup, watch her as she eats it, clear up when she finishes. She was obeying those instructions, unable to resist. It was rather sad, and reminded Emily of a fly batting against a window, following its urge to fly towards light, being caught out by the glass every time it clumped into it.

She'd almost finished the soup and, truth be told, she'd got bored of the game. The girl watched her still. Emily had come to hate her, with her bored expression and bovine eyes.

She dropped the bowl on the floor, and it broke into about a dozen pieces.

The girl's instructions covered this and she was down on the floor, collecting the bits faster than Emily would have given her credit for.

Emily had already selected one of the larger shards and slipped it into the single pocket of her overalls.

'Destiny,' Amanda told Radford, who was unhappy with the answer.

'It's too much of a coincidence,' he told her. 'You living here now, in London back in 1949. What are you really doing here?'

She smiled up at him. 'It's not a coincidence. It's the way things are, the way they have to be. The real question for you isn't what I'm doing here, it's what I will do in London, in your future.'

'The future?'

'Your future,' she corrected him.

Radford was flicking through her file. 'You were never a Party member. You fled London just before the purges started. You've led a charmed life.'

'I was told they were coming.'

'Really?'

'Yes.'

'A friend in the government? Simon Brown?'

'He lost his job before then.'

'So who tipped you off?'

Amanda smiled at him. 'You did. Back in 1949.' She reached into her overalls and handed Radford a faded envelope.

'What's this?'

'Open it.'

Radford did so.

'It's a letter. You gave it to me in 1949.'

'It's in my handwriting. It's a mission briefing.'

'I wouldn't know. I never opened it. You told me to deliver it to you today.'

Radford watched her warily. 'You remember me back in 1949?'

'Yes. Like you said. It's not a coincidence I am here.'

'At first we thought you'd retreated here to organise resistance. But you never contacted anyone, you never associated with anyone.'

Amanda looked pained. 'I was political once. It didn't work out the way I planned.' She hesitated. 'No, that's not true. We saw all this coming, you know. The revolution, the single party, the end of the class struggle. It was inevitable. The only question was precisely when and how, and if there was anything we could do to change the pace of that progress. We wished the revolution would come. Can you believe that? We wished the world would be like this.'

Radford wasn't listening, he was reading the mission briefing.

Lechasseur sat alone, strapped to the chair.

He'd been alone for a long time. He had no idea what the time was – and knew from a long convalescence a few years before how futile it was to guess. In circumstances like this, you measured time by when meals were served, when curtains were drawn, faint noises from outside. This room was windowless, and soundproof. No-one had been to see him since Ned and his son had left. The leather straps holding him to the chair weren't going anywhere, and – unlike the detectives in the movies – Lechasseur had lacked the foresight to conceal a knife on his person to hack them open.

He'd got a split lip, a black eye and (for the first time for a while) his old wounds were beginning to itch and ache. Ned had had no intention of killing Lechasseur, he had just wanted to hurt him. After only about three of four minutes he'd realised there was no sport in punching a man who was strapped down and couldn't lift his hand, let alone put up a fight.

The pain didn't bother Lechasseur. Not his own, anyway. Hands flat against the arms of the chair, he could

see them all – every previous person who'd sat in this chair. Men and women of all ages. No children, but at least one lad who was barely an adult. There was only one type of pain, here. The beating, the cosh, with only the occasional stabbing pain from a cigarette butt or knife. The same pain, repeated, not a unique torture. Lechasseur was merely the latest in a long line. Only three people had died here, and two of them had been very old. Like background noise or a foul smell, he was soon used to the landscape of pain he found himself in, and could block it out with little effort.

What was worrying him was that his mind was playing tricks. He was seeing the other reality again. Light streamed through non-existent windows. A fat man behind a desk was lecturing a Yorkshireman in a flat cap about efficient farming methods. They couldn't see the large, bloody, black man sitting within a few feet of them. Or if they could, they didn't mention it.

He found himself wishing Amanda was here. He liked her, he'd decided. Her crime had been naivety, and the wish to be a bit daring. It had, admittedly, resulted in the ruthless elimination of every aspect of life worth living, but he knew that deep down, she was a link to the old world. If he got away from here – which he wouldn't, he accepted – he'd make contact with her again.

Was Emily dead? The answer to that, of course, was that she was. He'd seen the body with his own eyes, and what more evidence did you need? By the same logic, Lechasseur realised he was probably dead, too. He'd be in his mid-sixties, so might be walking around somewhere in this future, but the wounds he'd got in Normandy must have shortened his life expectancy. If they hadn't, then a line of work that seemed increasingly to involve beatings and injuries would have done for him. Would a black foreigner really be allowed to exist in a future like this?

He found himself wondering how and when he'd died, rather than if he'd lived.

He'd not slept for a long time. Lechasseur found his eyelids were heavy. It was dark here, quiet, and there was nothing here but the pain and fear and hopelessness of those who'd come before him.

They cried out all around him, but not to him; they were oblivious to his presence. His head dipped to his chest, and he rested.

Radford tried to grab Emily. He was wearing a cheap suit, not his overalls. Why?

'We're going to 1949,' he told her.

'I don't understand.' She was cowering in the corner, now. The suit was his attempt to blend in, she realised. It couldn't possibly work, but neither would it draw attention to itself the way overalls would have. Radford was huge.

'It takes the two of us,' he explained. 'We think of somewhere, we go there. It's as simple as that. And it isn't a coincidence that you've been delivered here to me. It's the weight of history. It's inevitability.'

He handed her a piece of paper.

'I'm to contact Amanda, a woman I believe you're already acquainted with and – '

'Lechasseur met her, but – '

'I hand her an envelope. Money. She gives me some documents. State secrets. I then make sure they are delivered to some friends of hers. You're going to help me make history, Blandish.'

'But it doesn't work! We saw you . . . fighting in the street . . .'

Radford smiled. 'That's another thing to look forward to then . . . I wonder whether that was before or after I delivered the mail?'

He could snap her in two, she was sure of that.

He already had. The mere fact that she'd not been made to change out of her overalls and back into her 1949 clothes led to one conclusion – she wouldn't be blending in. She saw herself lying in the mud under Hammersmith Bridge.

'When I tell you to think of London, 1949, what do you think of?' he asked.

Emily opened her mouth to reply, , and Radford grabbed her shoulder

And then, on a cool, crisp, December night – for the merest moment – something happened that had been seen only twice before.

Emily and Radford were suddenly there, with just the faintest crackle of blue light.

After that, there was nothing unusual to see. She was dressed in thin, drab overalls that were too large, and overwhelmed her slight figure. She had long, chestnut hair. Her name was Emily Blandish. He was broad, shaven-headed; his suit had been made for him, and it just about looked like it. He was Radford.

He looked around, sniffed the air. If he noticed that she was shivering, he gave no sign of it.

'We're here?' he asked. 'We could be anywhere. You're sure we're here?'

'We're here,' she told him.

'How can you tell?'

'I don't know. But I can. It feels right.'

Radford shifted, leaving a fresh footprint. It hadn't occurred to him until that moment that there would be a set of tracks leading back to the shore, but no tracks down here. If anyone noticed that, they'd assume they'd arrived by boat. But that would have left impressions in the mud, too. Would that pique someone's curiosity? Lead them to ask questions?

The mud was already sucking itself flat where his first footprints had been, the evidence erasing itself.

He looked at Emily.

She slashed his face, aiming for his eyes, slicing his forehead instead.

'Forewarned is forearmed,' she said as he reeled.

She'd blinded him. No . . . it was blood. It ran down over his eyes, it was already around his nostrils and he could taste it on his top lip.

Emily hadn't run. She hadn't moved. So he reached out and punched her in the stomach. He heard her crash down into the mud, and advanced on her, wiping the blood away from his face.

She was laughing.

'I saw you before. You didn't have that scar when I saw you before, in the future, and believe me, you're going to have that scar for a while.'

He kicked her in the stomach. Incredibly, that just made her laugh more.

'That's going to be a nasty bruise. And I saw myself laid out on a slab and I didn't have a bruise on my stomach. I'm not going to die.'

Radford stamped on her head, holding it down in the mud.

'The precise detail of your death might have changed,' he told her. 'That's all.'

Emily was struggling. Her mouth and nose would be full of soft mud, now. Radford wiped some more blood from his forehead. He was feeling a little light-headed. He couldn't afford to let this last much longer.

'You're not going to die?' he mocked. 'Why are you struggling, then?'

He lifted his foot, and Emily spluttered and coughed.

'Answer me,' he shouted. 'You can't stop this. The Party will rise. It's happened.'

Emily slashed at his ankle with whatever it was in her hand. He screamed with pain.

She grabbed his leg, pulling him off balance.

If he went down, put a knee on her neck, he'd break it, or at the very least block her windpipe.

'Think of Lechasseur,' Emily suggested.

'Lechasseur?' Radford echoed.

Emily gripped him tighter, and they felt themselves slipping away.

Radford was fighting her. 'No.'

Blue energy was crackling all around them. 'I have to get back, and I need you for that. I'm going back for Lechasseur. And then I'll leave you where you belong.'

'No.'

'Without me, you can just sit in your office, seeing things.'

'You die. You have to die. You said it yourself: history has been written.'

'What can be written can be rewritten.'

Emily let go of Radford, who fell away, in a direction she couldn't begin to describe.

In his place was a ball of blue energy, surging towards her. Raw time, she thought, or maybe the sparks as time scraped its way across the universe. It was pushing at her, like an ocean wave.

She thought of Honoré Lechasseur, she thought of the manor house and she was there.

Lechasseur looked up to see Emily. She was wearing overalls, but he barely noticed that. She was both in the room and not, her feet firmly on the ground and a few inches in the air. There was a ring of blue energy around her. The ring of fire, the sense of something shielding him from light that should be blinding.

An angel.

She held out her hand, her electric wings spreading out behind her. He hesitated. This was such a beautiful dream, and he really didn't want to wake up.

'For God's sake, Honoré. We don't have long. Think about going home.'

He touched her hand and they vanished.

And, without Emily there, there was nothing blocking the light, and it shone in the cell, taking it apart, atom by atom, then spread through the whole of the house, blasting through the mortar, vaporising it, then pulling the bricks down from the cell one by one, crazing the glass, throwing the manor house, all its broken contents and inhabitants, out over its own lawns and the surrounding fields and woodlands. A moment later, the house was gone. All that was left were bricks sinking into the mud.

Lechasseur wondered how long it would be before the waiters would serve him. It felt like he'd been sitting in the little café for days.

Emily was opposite him, catching her breath.

They were in the café in the shadow of the British Museum. Any moment now, there would be gunshots.

The two of them held their breath, waiting. But it was quiet out there – or as quiet as London ever got.

'Did it happen?' Emily asked. She was in her dress, not overalls. She wasn't caked in mud and bruises. Lechasseur felt fine, if a little hungry.

'Why are you asking me?'

'You were there, too.'

'I guess that answers the question.'

Emily thought about it for a moment. 'I suppose . . . But if I didn't die, and Radford didn't come here . . .'

'That happened,' Lechasseur said. 'I remember it.'

'I died?' she asked, not needing to elaborate why she might disagree. 'It happened and it didn't? That doesn't add up.'

'Does it have to? We can agree what happened and what didn't,' Lechasseur said.

'I hope so.'

'What do you mean?'

'Is that the future? Is that what's going to happen?'

Lechasseur remembered the newspaper with its photograph of a female prime minister, a quiet country lane, strong tea in an unchipped mug.

'No,' he told her, almost as certain.

Emily cocked her head and listened. 'No gunshots . . . Who were those men anyway? Plain clothes police?'

'No idea. Maybe they got wind of what Brown was planning and were tailing him, and then when Amanda passed the documents to Radford, they followed him, and made their move too late to stop him passing them on.'

'But that never happened.'

'Appears not.'

Lechasseur looked around again. The waiters had already polished those glasses. He felt himself getting restless. It was odd. He ought to be tired, but it felt like he'd only just got up.

'Why aren't we sitting in here twice?' he asked. 'I remember sitting here before . . .'

Emily shrugged. 'I guess it's just what time does . . . heal itself.'

Lechasseur shook his head. 'Gives me a headache just thinking about it.'

Emily was watching him. 'Radford said that someone like me, and someone like you . . . when we touch, and think about going somewhere, we can go there. We can travel through time.'

Lechasseur looked at her levelly. 'Doesn't seem very likely.'

'Or very scientific.'

'I'll take your word for that.'

'But we both remember that it happened . . .'

Lechasseur looked at her. 'Yeah.'

'. . . and I think I remember doing it before . . .' Emily's eyes gazed into the distance as though she might be able to bring her memory back. 'There's something . . .' She sighed in frustration. 'Why can't I remember!'

Lechasseur gazed at her. 'You will . . . eventually. Give it time. Trust me, I know. Some scars take a long time to heal.'

She held out her hand, waved her fingers at him. Grinning.

'So where shall we go?'

'Somewhere they serve food. Somewhere with eggs.'

He took her hand.

ABOUT THE AUTHOR

Lance Parkin is the author of six *Doctor Who* novels, both for BBC Books and for Virgin Publishing. He also co-authored a novel featuring archaeologist Bernice Summerfield for Virgin, wrote a comprehensive guide to *Doctor Who*'s timeline (*A History of the Universe*) and is the author of several *Doctor Who* related audio and video releases. He was a storyline writer for the soap opera *Emmerdale* and edited the diaries of one of the characters from that show, penned a novel, *Emmerdale: Their Finest Hour*, as well as writing two factual books: *The Story of Emmerdale* and *30th Anniversary Emmerdale*. He has written a book about comics writer Alan Moore, a spin off book to the *Soapstars* TV series, and also a book about the *Star Trek* series, *Beyond The Final Frontier*.

ALSO AVAILABLE

TIME HUNTER

A range of high-quality original paperback novellas featuring the adventures in time of Honoré Lechasseur. Part mystery, part detective story, part dark fantasy, part science fiction . . . these books are guaranteed to enthrall fans of good fiction everywhere, and are in the spirit of our acclaimed range of *Doctor Who* Novellas.

THE TUNNEL AT THE END OF THE LIGHT
by STEFAN PETRUCHA

In the heart of post-war London, a bomb is discovered lodged at a disused station between Green Park and Hyde Park Corner. The bomb detonates, and as the dust clears, it becomes apparent that *something* has been awakened. Strange half-human creatures attack the workers at the site, hungrily searching for anything containing sugar . . .

Meanwhile, Honoré and Emily are contacted by eccentric poet Randolph Crest, who believes himself to be the target of these subterranean creatures. The ensuing investigation brings Honoré and Emily up against a terrifying force from deep beneath the earth, and one which even with their combined powers, they may have trouble stopping.

Stefan Petrucha is internationally acclaimed as the writer of Topps' *X-Files* comic. More recently, he's written the critical hit *Boston Blackie* for Moonstone's Noir Comics line and his dark fantasy novel, *Dark Ages: Assamite* from White Wolf Publishing, has just gone into a second printing.

120pp approx. A5 paperback original novella.
Available in standard paperback, or deluxe signed (by Petrucha) and numbered, limited edition hardback.
ISBN 1-903889-37-5 (pb) £7.99 UK $9.95 US $14.95 CAN
ISBN 1-903889-38-3 (hb) £25.00 UK $39.95 US $44.95 CAN
PUB: MARCH 2004 (UK) JUNE 2004 (US/CAN)

THE CLOCKWORK WOMAN by CLAIRE BOTT

Honoré and Emily find themselves imprisoned in the late 19th Century by a celebrated inventor . . . but help comes from an unexpected source – a humanoid automaton created by and to give pleasure to its owner. As the trio escape to London, they are unprepared for what awaits them, and at every turn it seems impossible to avert what fate may have in store for the Clockwork Woman.
120pp approx. A5 paperback original novella.
Available in standard paperback, or deluxe signed (by Bott) and numbered, limited edition hardback.
ISBN 1-903889-39-1 (pb) £7.99 UK $9.95 US $14.95 CAN
ISBN 1-903889-40-5 (hb) £25.00 UK $39.95 US $44.95 CAN
PUB: JUNE 2004 (UK) SEPTEMBER 2004 (US/CAN)

DOCTOR WHO

DOCTOR WHO: TIME AND RELATIVE by KIM NEWMAN

The harsh British winter of 1962/3 brings a big freeze and with it comes a new, far greater menace: terrifying icy creatures are stalking the streets, bringing death and destruction.
An adventure featuring the first Doctor and Susan.
Featuring a foreword by Justin Richards.
Deluxe edition frontispiece by Bryan Talbot.
SOLD OUT Standard h/b ISBN: 1-903889-02-2
£25 (+ £1.50 UK p&p) Deluxe h/h ISBN: 1 903009-03-0

DOCTOR WHO: CITADEL OF DREAMS by DAVE STONE

In the city-state of Hokesh, time plays tricks; the present is unreliable, the future impossible to intimate.
An adventure featuring the seventh Doctor and Ace.

Featuring a foreword by Andrew Cartmel.
Deluxe edition frontispiece by Lee Sullivan.
£10 (+ £1.50 UK p&p) Standard h/b ISBN: 1-903889-04-9
£25 (+ £1.50 UK p&p) Deluxe h/b ISBN: 1-903889-05-7

DOCTOR WHO: NIGHTDREAMERS by TOM ARDEN

Perihelion Night on the wooded moon Verd. A time of strange sightings, ghosts, and celebration. But what of the mysterious and terrifying Nightdreamers? And of the Nightdreamer King?
An adventure featuring the third Doctor and Jo.
Featuring a foreword by Katy Manning.
Deluxe edition frontispiece by Martin McKenna.
£10 (+ £1.50 UK p&p) Standard h/b ISBN: 1-903889-06-5
£25 (+ £1.50 UK p&p) Deluxe h/b ISBN: 1-903889-07-3

DOCTOR WHO: GHOST SHIP by KEITH TOPPING

The TARDIS lands in the most haunted place on Earth, the luxury ocean liner the Queen Mary on its way from Southampton to New York in the year 1963. But why do ghosts from the past, the present and, perhaps even the future, seek out the Doctor?
An adventure featuring the fourth Doctor.
Featuring a foreword by Hugh Lamb.
Deluxe edition frontispiece by Dariusz Jasiczak.
£5.99 (+ £1.50 UK p&p) p/b ISBN: 1-903889-32-4
SOLD OUT Standard h/b ISBN: 1-903889-08-1
£25 (+ £1.50 UK p&p) Deluxe h/b ISBN: 1-903889-09-X

DOCTOR WHO: FOREIGN DEVILS by ANDREW CARTMEL

The Doctor, Jamie and Zoe find themselves joining forces with a psychic investigator named Carnacki to solve a series of strange murders in an English country house.
An adventure featuring the second Doctor, Jamie and Zoe.
Featuring a foreword by Mike Ashley.
Deluxe edition frontispiece by Mike Collins.
£5.99 (+ £1.50 UK p&p) p/b ISBN: 1-903889-33-2
SOLD OUT Standard h/b ISBN: 1-903889-10-3
£25 (+ £1.50 UK p&p) Deluxe h/b ISBN: 1-903889-11-1

DOCTOR WHO: RIP TIDE by LOUISE COOPER

Strange things are afoot in a sleepy Cornish village. Strangers are hanging about the harbour and a mysterious object is retrieved from the sea bed. Then the locals start getting sick. The Doctor is perhaps the only person who can help, but can he discover the truth in time?

An adventure featuring the eighth Doctor.
Featuring a foreword by Stephen Gallagher.
Deluxe edition frontispiece by Fred Gambino.
£10 (+ £1.50 UK p&p) Standard h/b ISBN: 1-903889-12-X
£25 (+ £1.50 UK p&p) Deluxe h/b ISBN: 1-903889-13-8

DOCTOR WHO: WONDERLAND by MARK CHADBOURN

San Francisco 1967. A place of love and peace as the hippy movement is in full swing. Summer, however, has lost her boyfriend, and fears him dead, destroyed by a new type of drug nicknamed Blue Moonbeams. Her only friends are three English tourists: Ben and Polly, and the mysterious Doctor. But will any of them help Summer, and what is the strange threat posed by the Blue Moonbeams?

An adventure featuring the second Doctor, Ben and Polly.
Featuring a foreword by Graham Joyce.
Deluxe edition frontispiece by Dominic Harman.
£10 (+ £1.50 UK p&p) Standard h/b ISBN: 1-903889-14-6
£25 (+ £1.50 UK p&p) Deluxe h/b ISBN: 1-903889-15-4

DOCTOR WHO: SHELL SHOCK by SIMON A. FORWARD

The Doctor is stranded on an alien beach with only intelligent crabs and a madman for company. How can he possibly rescue Peri, who was lost at sea the same time as he and the TARDIS?

An adventure featuring the sixth Doctor and Peri.
Featuring a foreword by Guy N. Smith.
Deluxe edition frontispiece by Bob Covington.
£10 (+ £1.50 UK p&p) Standard h/b ISBN. 1-903889-16-2
£25 (+ £1.50 UK p&p) Deluxe h/b ISBN: 1-903889-17-0

DOCTOR WHO: THE CABINET OF LIGHT by DANIEL O'MAHONY

Where is the Doctor? Everyone is hunting him. Honoré Lechasseur, a time sensitive 'fixer', is hired by mystery woman Emily Blandish to find

him. But what is his connection with London in 1949? Lechasseur is about to discover that following in the Doctor's footsteps can be a difficult task.
An adventure featuring the Doctor.
Featuring a foreword by Chaz Brenchley.
Deluxe edition frontispiece by John Higgins.
£10 (+ £1.50 UK p&p) Standard h/b ISBN: 1-903889-18-9
£25 (+ £1.50 UK p&p) Deluxe h/b ISBN: 1-903889-19-7

DOCTOR WHO: FALLEN GODS
by KATE ORMAN & JONATHAN BLUM
In ancient Akrotiri, a young girl is learning the mysteries of magic from a tutor, who, quite literally, fell from the skies. With his encouragement she can surf the timestreams and see something of the future. But then the demons come.
An adventure featuring the eighth Doctor
Featuring a foreword by Storm Constantine.
Deluxe edition frontispiece by Daryl Joyce.
£10 (+ £1.50 UK p&p) Standard h/b ISBN: 1-903889-20-1
£25 (+ £1.50 UK p&p) Deluxe h/b ISBN: 1-903889-21-9

DOCTOR WHO: FRAYED by TARA SAMMS
On a blasted world, the Doctor and Susan find themselves in the middle of a war they cannot understand. With Susan missing and the Doctor captured, who will save the people from the enemies from both outside and within?
An adventure featuring the first Doctor and Susan.
Featuring a foreword by Stephen Laws.
Deluxe edition frontispiece by Chris Moore.
£10 (+ £1.50 UK p&p) Standard h/b ISBN: 1-903889-22-7
£25 (+ £1.50 UK p&p) Deluxe h/b ISBN: 1-903889-23-5

HORROR/FANTASY

THE MANITOU by GRAHAM MASTERTON
A 25th Anniversary author's preferred edition of this classic horror novel. An ancient Red Indian medicine man is reincarnated in modern day New York intent on reclaiming his land from the white men.

£9.99 (+ £2.50 p&p) Standard p/b ISBN: 1-903889-70-7
£30.00 (+ £2.50 p&p) Deluxe h/b ISBN: 1-903889-71-5

CAPE WRATH by PAUL FINCH
On a deserted Scottish island an ancient Viking warrior chief returns to life.
£8.00 (+ £1.50 p&p) Standard p/b ISBN: 1-903889-60-X

KING OF ALL THE DEAD by STEVE LOCKLEY & PAUL LEWIS
The king of all the dead will have what is his.
£8.00 (+ £1.50 p&p) Standard p/b ISBN: 1-903889-61-8

GUARDIAN ANGEL by STEPHANIE BEDWELL-GRIME
Devilish fun as Guardian Angel Porsche Winter loses a soul to the devil . . .
£9.99 (+ £2.50 p&p) Standard p/b ISBN: 1-903889-62-6

ASPECTS OF A PSYCHOPATH by ALISTAIR LANGSTON
Goes deeper than ever before into the twisted psyche of a serial killer. Horrific, graphic and gripping, this book is not for the squeamish.
£8.00 (+ £1.50 p&p) Standard p/b ISBN: 1-903889-63-4

SPECTRE by STEPHEN LAWS
The inseparable Byker Chapter: six boys, one girl, growing up together in the back streets of Newcastle. Now memories are all that Richard Eden has left, and one treasured photograph. But suddenly, inexplicably, the images of his companions start to fade, and as they vanish, so his friends are found dead and mutilated. Something is stalking the Chapter, picking them off one by one, something connected with their past, and with the girl they used to know.
£9.99 (+ £2.50 p&p) Standard p/b ISBN: 1-903889-72-3
£30.00 (+ £2.50 p&p) Deluxe h/b ISBN: 1-903889-73-1

TV/FILM GUIDES

BEYOND THE GATE: THE UNOFFICIAL AND UNAUTHORISED GUIDE TO STARGATE SG-1 by KEITH TOPPING
Complete episode guide to the middle of Season 6 of the popular TV show.
£9.99 (+ £2.50 p&p) Standard p/b ISBN: 1-903889-50-2

A DAY IN THE LIFE: THE UNOFFICIAL AND UNAUTHORISED GUIDE TO 24 by KEITH TOPPING
Complete episode guide to the first season of the popular TV show.
£9.99 (+ £2.50 p&p) Standard p/b ISBN: 1-903889-53-7

THE TELEVISION COMPANION: THE UNOFFICIAL AND UNAUTHORISED GUIDE TO DOCTOR WHO by DAVID J HOWE & STEPHEN JAMES WALKER
Complete episode guide to the popular TV show.
£14.99 (+ £4.00 p&p) Standard p/b ISBN: 1-903889-51-0
£30.00 (+ £4.00 p&p) Deluxe h/b ISBN: 1-903889-52-9

LIBERATION: THE UNOFFICIAL AND UNAUTHORISED GUIDE TO BLAKE'S 7 by ALAN STEVENS & FIONA MOORE
Complete episode guide to the popular TV show.
Featuring a foreword by David Maloney
£9.99 (+ £2.50 p&p) Standard p/b ISBN: 1-903889-54-5
£30.00 (+ £2.50 p&p) Deluxe h/b ISBN: 1-903889-55-3

HANK JANSON
Classic pulp crime thrillers from the 1950s.

TORMENT by HANK JANSON
£9.99 (+ £2.50 p&p) Standard p/b ISBN: 1-903889-80-4
WOMEN HATE TILL DEATH by HANK JANSON
£9.99 (+ £2.50 p&p) Standard p/b ISBN: 1-903889-81-2

The prices shown are correct at time of going to press. However, the publishers reserve the right to increase prices from those previously advertised without prior notice.

TELOS PUBLISHING c/o Beech House, Chapel Lane, Moulton, Cheshire, CW9 8PQ, England
Email: orders@telos.co.uk • Web: www.telos.co.uk

To order copies of any Telos books, please visit our website where there are full details of all titles and facilities for worldwide credit card online ordering, or send a cheque or postal order (UK only) for the appropriate amount (including postage and packing), together with details of the book(s) you require, plus your name and address to the above address. Overseas readers please send two international reply coupons for details of prices and postage rates.